새

도서출판 아시아에서는 《바이링궐 에디션 한국 대표 소설》을 기획하여 한국의 우수한 문학을 주제별로 엄선해 국내외 독자들에게 소개합니다. 이 기획은 국내외 우수한 번역가들이 참여하여 원작의 품격을 최대한 살렸습니다. 문학을 통해 아시아의 정체성과 가치를 살피는 데 주력해 온 도서출판 아시아는 한국인의 삶을 넓고 깊게 이해하는 데 이 기획이 기여하기를 기대합니다.

Asia Publishers presents some of the very best modern Korean literature to readers worldwide through its new Korean literature series ⟨Bilingual Edition Modern Korean Literature⟩. We are proud and happy to offer it in the most authoritative translation by renowned translators of Korean literature. We hope that this series helps to build solid bridges between citizens of the world and Koreans through a rich in-depth understanding of Korea.

바이링궐 에디션 한국 대표 소설 **057**

Bi-lingual Edition Modern Korean Literature 057

Bird

전성태
새

Jeon Sung-tae

ASIA
PUBLISHERS

Contents

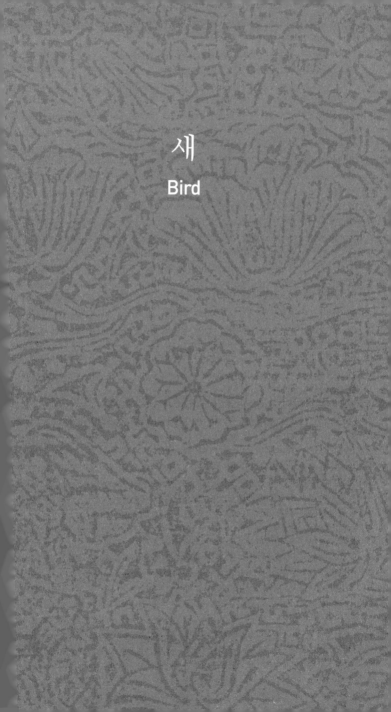

새
Bird

요것을 무슨 수로 내돌릴까?

방 안을 좀 엿보자고 볕이 창턱에 걸터앉았으니 아침
도 한참은 지났으련만 저것은 무슨 배짱으로 여기서 여
태 자빠져 자고 있느냔 말이다. 부지런한 동네 눈들이
죄 밖으로 기어나왔을 텐데…….

집은 한갓지게 문대미골 꼭대기에 앉아 있다. 마을 건
너 골짜기에 담긴 저수지까지 앞마당으로 삼았으니 눈
길은 시원해 좋지만 집 안은 숨길 데 없이 훤하였다. 손
바닥만한 마당 너머로는 울도 없이 곧장 남의 배밭이요
배나무들은 발라먹은 개뼈다귀처럼 헐벗었다. 집 나간
여편네를 둔 사내로 입길에 오르내리는 처지에 무슨 체

How can I get her out of here, Su-dong thought.

The sunlight peeked just over the windows. It must have already been mid-morning. How on earth could this bitch still be sleeping? All the watchful eyes of the neighborhood must have already been out.

His house sat quietly atop Mundaemigol. It was high up and overlooked nearly the entire neighborhood. One could even consider the reservoir in the valley on the other side of the village his front yard. The location was good for its view, but his house was completely exposed to the preying eyes of the other villagers. Beyond its palm-sized yard, there was his neighbor's fenceless pear orchard

면 걱정이냐 싶으나 그래도 수동은 술집 여자를 제 안방으로 끌어들인 망나니라는 꼬리표까지 달고 싶진 않았다.

"어이!"

수동은 밍근한 물주전자를 입에서 떼며 발끝으로 여자의 엉덩이를 꾸욱 밀었다. 아웅, 여자는 잠투정 같은 소리를 찔끔 흘리곤 캐시밀론 이불 속으로 미끄러져 들 뿐이다. 더럽게 꼬였다! 다 된 밥에 콧물을 흘려도 유분수지 오늘같이 중한 날 이 무슨 낭패냐.

"어이, 싸게 일어나줘야 쓰겄어."

요번엔 요강단지 밀어놓듯 볼기짝을 썩 거칠게 밀어붙인다. 그제야 여자는 부스스한 얼굴을 이불 밖으로 내놓는다. 화장 지워진 얼굴은 오래된 회벽처럼 볼썽사납다. 조명발 아래서는 달랑달랑한 스물아홉이라고 속살대더니 말짱 거짓이었나 보다. 마흔까지 넘겨보아도 무리 없겠다.

"몇 시야?"

눈가에 몰렸던 괴로운 표정이 입가로 떨어져 일그러지는 것이 저도 속깨나 쓰린 모양이다. 하긴 과하긴 했다. 도대체 몇 시까지 부은 술이냐. 수동은 주전자를 여

that demarcated the boundaries between them. The pear trees were entirely naked, like bones that had been stripped clean by a dog. Everyone thought his wife had run away on him anyways, so he didn't have to worry too much about his reputation. Still, Su-dong didn't want the label of being the kind of ass who invited barmaids into his bedroom night after night.

"Hey!" Su-dong said. He prodded the woman's bottom with the tips of his toes. As he tried to nudge her awake he took the spout off of a lukewarm water kettle with his teeth.

"Hmmm," she said. The woman murmured something indecipherable like a baby peevishly speaking in its sleep. She burrowed her way deeper into the comforter. What a drag this day was turning into. What a disaster—and on today of all days! It is like dunking your nose into a cup of coffee before you're even able to get that first sip.

"Hey, please, let's go!"

This time, he jabbed her rear end as if he was giving a chamber pot a gentle boot. Finally, she brought her disheveled face out from under the comforter. She no longer had any makeup on and her face looked as ugly as an old plaster wall. Un-

자 앞으로 밀어놓는다.

"내 안경."

수동은 브래지어 옆에 뒹구는 테가 붉은 안경까지 착실하게 밀어준다. 정양은 시력이 좋다. 한데도 안경을 착용하는 것은 순전히 직업의식의 발로란다. 뭐 시골뜨기들은 지적(知的)으로 뵈는 여자 앞에서는 맥을 못 춘다나.

"직업의식이 왜 그리 흐릿혀? 좀 작신작신 녹여놓으란 놈은 어디다가 내불고 여서 드러누웠어! 기왕 그랬대도 해 나기 전에는 사라져줬어야 쓸 거 아니라고."

"어머! 말씀하시는 것 좀 봐. 뭣 주고 뺨 맞는다더니……."

여자는 말끝 삼킨 주둥아리에 더듬어 찾은 담배를 쑤셔 박는다. 호필이도 한데 어울려 자다가 갔는가? 그러나 흔적은 없다.

찰거머리 같은 진구, 호필이 놈들을 따돌리느라고 마련한 술자리였다. 녀석들은 친구라고도 할 수 없을 만치 돈푼에 사람을 아주 잡으려고 든다. 누가 연대보증인들 아니랄까봐 똘똘 뭉쳐 친구의 도주를 감시하고 드는 게 아예 형사들 뺨친다. 특히 호필이는 트럭까지 압

der the artificial lighting last night, she had whispered that she was only twenty-nine, but it was clear now that she had lied. Clearly, she was considerably over forty.

"What time is it?" she said.

She had a painful expression on her face that shifted from around her eyes to the area around her mouth: she must have had some sort of stomach ache. There was no denying that they had drunk too much. Why did they stay out so late drinking? Su-dong pushed the kettle in her direction.

"My glasses."

Su-dong courteously nudged the red-rimmed glasses lying near the woman's bra towards her. Miss Jeong's eyesight was good. She said that she wore the glasses only for the sake of professionalism. According to her, country bumpkins melted like ice on hot summer days in front of intellectual-looking women.

"What happened to your professionalism?" Su-dong asked. "Where did you drop the guy I told you to go home with? And now you're lying here? Even if you had to, you still should've been gone by sunrise."

수해 가서 발을 묶어놓고 운신을 못하게 한다. 각시 찾으러 나간다고 둘러대도 주변머리없이 함께 나서겠다고나 할까 통 내놓질 않는다. 술자리에서 호필이 옆에 정양을 붙여놓은 것도 다 그 때문인데, 원수 같은 술 때문에 일이 다 뻐그러진 모양이다.

"아, 시방 입구녕에 불때고 누웠을 때가 아니래두 그러네. 대체 지난밤 스케줄은 어떻게 꼬인 거여?"

그래도 여자는 듣는 둥 만 둥이다. 몸을 벌렁 돌려 눕곤 담배연기를 천장까지 올릴 기세로 뿜다가 흥, 내지르는 게 콧방귀다.

"스케줄이 무슨 빤스 고무줄이대?"

하다 말고 여자는 불쑥 담배 든 쪽 손목을 코앞에 내밀어놓는다. 강낭콩 꽃잎 같은 멍 두 장이 푸른 실핏줄 위에 선명하게 피어 있다. 듣지 않아도 술자리 끝은 뻔하다. 정작엔 수동 자신이 못 쓰게 취해서 호필이를 밀어내고 정양의 손목을 잡아끌었으리라.

"이별하는 마당에 아쉽다고 좋게 한 코 달래지 우악스럽긴……"

이별이라는 말이 웬일인지 도주로만 들려 수동은 뜨끔하다. 달이 차서 정양이 떠날 때가 되었다는 소린 줄

"Whoa whoa whoa! Listen to what you're saying. I guess what they say is true. No one good deed ever goes unpunished..." She slurred the last part of that sentence and then groped for a cigarette and shoved it into her mouth. Had Ho-pil slept here, too? Su-dong could not find any trace that he had been here.

Su-dong had treated Jin-gu and Ho-pil to a night of drinking last night because they had been following him around, clinging to him like a pair of ticks. They almost didn't deserve to be called his friends considering how they had treated him over just a little money. As if to show exactly what it really meant to be "co-signers," they remained fiercely united in keeping an eye on Su-dong lest he run away. They were more passionate and diligent than a pair of detectives. Ho-pil had even taken Su-dong's truck to prevent him from running. Even when Su-dong cooked up the excuse of going to search for his runaway wife, the clueless Ho-pil had volunteered to go with him and had ended up not even giving him his truck back.

That was why he had sat Miss Jeong next to Ho-pil at last night's drinking party. But it looked like he had messed it all up thanks to his worst enemy:

뻔히 알면서도 도둑이 제 발 저린 꼴이다. 어쨌든 피차 이별이긴 이별인 셈이다. 다만 저는 근무지를 옮겨 앉는 것이고 수동 자신은 볼 장 다 보고 튀자는 마당이니 감회야 같을 수 없다. 객지 어느 뒷골목에서 서로 또 맞닥뜨린다면 감방 식구 만난 것보다 더 껄끄러우리라. 수동은 피식 웃고 만다.

"외상값 수금 전엔 나도 여기서 요양이나 할 셈야. 어젯밤은 서비스로 치지 뭐."

"정 떨어지게 시방 왜 이러서?"

"흥, 자기야말로 정 들게 왜 그러시는데?"

퐁 퐁 퐁 담배연기만 오른다.

수동은 당겨 앉는다. 이불을 들추고 푸실푸실한 여자의 엉덩이를 토닥이며,

"땅값 나오는 대로 내 갚는대도 그런다."

하나, 여자는 이불 빼앗듯 몸을 저쪽으로 휘뚝 뒤집어 버린다. 한 가닥 창틈으로 흘러든 햇살 기둥이 뽀얘지게 먼지만 일었다. 맥맥한 노릇이다.

"흥, 곧곧 하시던 게 벌써 석 달째셔. 거긴 오십만 원을 땅에 심어났나 봐. 움트고 잎 달고 가지에 열려야 끊어줄 모양이지? 전근 가야 할 몸이 거기 땜에 열흘이나

liquor.

"Oh, it's not time for you to just lie there and smoke with that muzzle of yours. What the hell happened last night? What'd you do to ruin all my plans?"

Miss Jeong paid no attention to Su-dong. Barely budging at all from her position on the bed, she lazily turned herself over and blew cigarette smoke up at the ceiling.

"What plans? Plans to kick your ass?" she retorted.

She thrust her wrist right under Su-dong's nose. Two bruises were blooming like haricot bean flower petals above a line of thin blue veins. He did not have to be reminded what had happened at the end of the previous night's drinking party. Most likely, Su-dong himself must have been extremely drunk and had pushed Ho-pil away to drag Miss Jeong away by her wrist.

"You should have just said that you'd like to have me once before leaving. My, you're rough!"

As "leaving" sounded a lot like "running away" to Su-dong, he began to feel guilty. Although he very well knew that she meant that it was time for her to leave, he still felt guilty because "a guilty con-

매였다구."

정말 여기서 죽칠 셈인가? 어떻게든 살살 녹여서 제 발로 나가게 하는 수밖에 없을 것 같다. 수동은 일단 여자의 허구리를 더듬으며 파고들어본다.

"어머머!"

급습을 당한 여자는 발버둥을 친다. 내친김에 손 하나를 깍지 끼어 묶고 가슴으론 짓누르며 "우리 사이가…… 으디…… 그깟 푼돈으로 맺어진……" 하며 또 노는 손으로는 맨살을 더듬어 내려가다가 "읍, 뜨거!" 수동은 뒤로 벌렁 나자빠졌다. 담배 불똥에 그만 손등을 지지고 만 것이다.

"갈 테야!"

여자가 벌떡 일어나 앉는다. 핏, 진작에 그럴 일이다. 수동은 덴 자리에 침을 발랐다. 이불을 먼지 나게 들춘 여자가 속옷에 두 발을 담그자, 수동은 입꼬리를 올리며 문구멍에다가 눈을 박았다.

볕이 쨍글쨍글하다. 먼데로는 아지랑이가 자욱이 피어올라 눈에 백태라도 낀 것 같다. 볕도 여물어 군불 지피듯 하고 사날 전에는 한 줄금 빗방울마저 비쳤으니 오늘내일 나무 몸뚱어리마다 움들이 터질 것이다. 땅을

science needs no accuser," as the saying goes. At any rate, it was "leaving" for both of them for sure. But, Miss Jeong had simply been moving from one line of work to the next while Su-dong was running away entirely. So, their feelings weren't exactly comparable. If he ran into her in some alley in the future, he imagined he would feel even more uncomfortable than a former prisoner running into an old prison mate. Su-dong chuckled at himself.

"I'm gonna take a nap here until I get all the money owed to me. I'll consider last night a favor," Miss Jeong said.

"Why are you doing this? I'm feeling like I'm falling out of love with you." Su-dong smiled down at her.

"Oh? Why are you doing *that*? To make me fall in love with you?" She blew more cigarette smoke up at him.

Su-dong came closer to her, and, lifting the comforter, patted her on her plump bottom.

"I said I'll pay you as soon as I get paid for my property," Su-dong said.

But Miss Jeong just turned away from him and snatched the comforter away. She raised some dust as she turned away and it blurred the shaft of sun-

뒤집어 골라놓은 배밭은 겉흙이 푸슬푸슬 메말랐다. 그러고 보니 자갈에 괭잇날 부딪는 소리가 아까부터 있었다. 두릿거려 보지만 등걸처럼 뭉툭하게 선 배나무 아래 어디에도 밭 임자는 없고 모듬모듬 쌓아둔 돌무더기만 부시다. 층층이 마을 가운데까지 흘러내린 밭은 맨 그런 배밭 아니면 마늘밭이다. 남들은 겨울 산천초목이 황량하고 으스산하네 해쌌지만 수동은 왠지 요맘때가 제일 그래 보인다.

마을에서 날선 빛이 날아와 눈을 찌른다. 아이 업은 노인네 하나가 회관에 딸린 경로당 문을 당기고 들어간다. "출근들을 하시는군." 중얼거리며 수동은 담배를 물었다.

저수지로 빠지는 조금돌이길로도 남녀가 섞인 댓 명이 경운기에 올라 있다. 저수지로 공공근로를 나가는 품꾼들이다. 호필이도 끼였을까? 멀어서 알 수 없다. 놈도 밤새 술에 몸을 씻었으니 아직 구들장을 못 벗었을 테지. 점심참까지만 엎어져 있거라.

어쨌든 여자를 내보내려면 저 눈들을 피해야 한다. 눈이 침침한 노인네들이라고 무시해서는 큰코다친다. 골목에 얼쩡거리는 개도 뉘집 개인지 척 알아낼 판이니

20

light entering through the crack in the window. He felt helpless.

"Huh, it's been three months since you told me you'd repay me right away. You must have buried the fifty thousand *won*. Are you waiting for it to come out of the ground, sprout leaves, and grow fruit? And then pick the fruit-money and give it to me? I should have been at my new work ten days ago. You're the one who's holding me up here."

Is she really going to stay here? There seemed no other way to make her go other than to sweet-talk her into leaving on her own. Su-dong put his hands on her waist, burrowing underneath the comforter himself.

"Goodness me!"

Surprised, Miss Jeon began to writhe. Su-dong went ahead and clasped her fingers tight with one of his hands. He then put a hand on one of her breasts and said, "Our relationship...is more than...just about a little money." He began to grope her naked body with his other hand until he fell out of the bed backwards with a cry. The back of his hand had been burned by the embers of her cigarette.

"Fine, I'll go!" Miss Jeong cried.

이 말만한 여자를 회관 앞길로 내돌리기란 여간한 일이 아니다. 잠시 생각에 골똘해 있던 수동은 스커트마저 다 끌어올린 여자에게,

"잠, 기둘려이."

해놓고 장롱 문을 연다. 아내의 옷가지 중에 남은 게 좀 있을 게다. 집 떠날 때 가방을 단출하게 싸라고 윽박을 놓았으니 말이다. 아내는 하나라도 더 챙기려고 장롱 앞에서 꾸물거렸다.

"도망치는 여편네가 옷 보따리는 다 뭐여?"

"나가 은제 도망쳐봤어? 그라고 갖고 갈 옷가지가 있기나 해?"

하긴 언제 옷 한 벌 사준 적이 있었던가. 맨 아이 옷에다가 제 것이라고는 살림 들어올 때 가져온 것하고 장날 한두 벌 싼 맛에 들여놓은 것들뿐이다.

"그람 참말로 바람나서 도망쳬부까."

서글픈 마음을 다잡자고 해 본 소리였겠지만 그렇게 단단한 아내가 그저껫밤에 살짝 전화를 넣어서는 꿀쩍꿀쩍 눈물을 짰다.

"은제 온데? 근호가 자꾸 아빠를 찾는디. 나도 불편하고."

Miss Jeong sat up. Gosh, and why didn't you just go before? Su-dong licked his fresh burn. After lifting the comforter and raising more dust, she put her two feet through her underwear. His mouth widening, Su-dong stared out through a hole in the door.

The sun was intense. Far away, the heat was radiating through the air so much that it felt like his eyeballs were burning from some kind of disease. The sun was heating the air. Since there had been showers a few days ago, the trees would begin to sprout in a day or two. The pear orchard had just been plowed and was beginning to show the dried and crumbling earth. Su-dong realized just then that he had been hearing the sound of the pickaxe hitting stone for some time now. He looked around, but he could not see the pear orchard owner anywhere under the pear trees, all of the trees looking blunt and stunted like stumps. It was only the mounds of stone that dazzled brightly here and there. There were layers upon layers of pear orchards or garlic fields sloping down towards the village center. Although people said that the winter scenery was desolate and gloomy, Su-dong felt that it was around this time when nature

"뭐가 불편하다고 난리여! 생판 노므 집도 아닌디. 일 매듭짓는 대루 금방 간다니께."

아내는 순천역 앞에서 여관을 하는 제 이모네에 잠시 얹혔다. 불편하긴 할 것이다. 여관이 좀 드센 곳이며 이 모래야 뜨내기손님들을 상대로 늙어선지 잔정은 닳고 없는 노파였다. 그러나마나 오늘만 지나면 안팎으로 고생 끝이다. 나주(羅州) 사람을 만나 땅문서를 넘기면 바로 서울이나 그 어름으로 튈 것이다. 약속한 시간이 열한 시. 시간은 어느새 버뜩 코앞에 다가와 있다.

여름 옷가지는 더러 눈에 띄는데 소매 긴 것들은 통 보이지 않는다. 좀생이 같은 여편네, 기어이 다 젊어지고 갔구나. 그래도 다행히 일할 때 입던 풍덩한 몸뻬바지와 솜을 누빈 조끼가 남아 있다.

"어머! 그건 왜?"

여자는 기겁을 한다. 장롱에서 돈 나올 줄 알았을 터인데 도떼기시장 물건 같은 것들이 쏟아지니 그럴 만하다.

"어디 동네에 광고할 일 있어? 잔말 말고 걸쳐봐."

"그걸 입으면 더 우셋거리지. 그리고 우세 살 건 또 뭐 있어? 나야 퇴근하는 길인데 뭐."

"이 장수동이하고 놀아난 걸 눈들이 알믄 나야 괜찮

looked the most depressing.

The sunlight flared up into Su-dong's house from the village and flashed into his eyes. An elderly woman pulled open the door of the senior center adjacent to the village office building and went inside, with a baby on her back.

"As punctual as if they're going to work." Su-dong stuck a cigarette into his mouth.

A group of five or six men and women were on a cultivator going up the gently bending, inclined road to the reservoir. They were day laborers going to a public works location. Would Ho-pil be there? They were too far away for Su-dong to tell. Ho-pil had bathed in liquor last night and so he probably wouldn't have unglued his backside from off the floor just yet. *Please just stay there until around lunch.*

At any rate, if he was going to send Miss Jeong away, he had to avoid their stares. If he just ignored them, treating them as if they were just blind and old, he wouldn't hear the end of it. They would immediately recognize whose house a dog lingering in an alley belonged to. So, it would not do to send this woman, as big as a horse, out in front of the village office building carelessly.

다만 너는 고별사 댕기는 마당에 얼굴 못 들 거인디."

"칫, 소갈머리는 틔었네."

그래도 여자는 분첩이나 토닥일까 걸레 밀쳐놓듯 옷가지는 저만치다. 입술을 말아 빼고 붉은 루주까지 한 바퀴 주욱 돌리곤 태평스레 쩝쩝한다.

"하, 헛손질 말어! 이 옷에 시방 어쩌자는 분장이여."

버썩 속이 탄 수동은 루주와 분첩을 빼앗아 핸드백에 처넣는다.

"싫다니까! 그것 안 입으려고 이 촌구석으로 굴러온 나야."

"용케 동네만 벗어나믄 시궁창에 처녀믄 된대두 그런다."

"당장 내 신세가 시궁창 신세가 되게 생겼으니 하는 말이지."

말기운이 다소 으츠러지긴 했지만 여자는 여전히 뚱해 앉았다.

수동은 몸뻬바지를 품에 안겨준다. 적갈색 바탕에 호박꽃인지 목단인지 누리끼리한 꽃이 넝쿨졌다. 여자는 걸레 다루듯 바지를 홀홀 털어 펼친다.

"돌아앉아 있어."

After pondering this for a while, Su-dong told her to wait a minute, although she had already tugged her skirt back on.

He opened his wardrobe. He should have had some of his wife's clothes left; he had yelled at her to pack her bag light. In the end his wife had lingered in front of the wardrobe in order to pack as much as possible.

"You're supposed to be running away. Why pack all these clothes?" Su-dong had snapped at her.

"Does this look like something I've ever done before?" his wife had answered.

"Anyways," she snapped, "what clothes do I even have to pack?"

It was true that he hadn't ever bought her clothes. The only things she'd ended up packing were their son's clothes and her own clothes, most of which—except for a couple of articles she'd bought cheap at fairs—she had brought with her when they moved in together.

"Maybe I really should have an affair and run away?"

Su-dong's wife must have said this to keep a handle on her feelings. His wife, ordinarily so strong, had called him two nights ago sobbing.

27

"벨꼴이시. 속옷도 훌렁훌렁 잘 벗고 입는 아가……."

수동은 문을 찌긋이 열어놓고 담배에 불을 붙여 문다. 동네에 생선 장사꾼이라도 들었는지 아싸아싸 하는 가락이 골목길 휘어진 대로 솟았다간 시든다. 저 아싸는 그저 제가 마이크 잡고 한 바퀴 돌려야만 제격이지 앉아 듣기에는 그보다 방정맞은 가락도 없다.

"사모님이 되게 풍채가 좋으셨나봐."

여자가 헐렁한 몸뻬바지 허리춤을 그러쥐고 한 바퀴 돌아본다. 정양만한 몸은 둘씩을 담고도 남을 만치 풍덩하다. 여자들은 그 품이 그 품이려니 했더니 의외다. 아내는 여고 다닐 때 투포환 대표선수였다. 손바닥이 솥뚜껑만하여 잡는 재미라곤 별로 없어 연애시절에 두어 번 잡아봤을까 그 뒤론 발 대하듯이 하였다. 그 손바닥으로 아이를 때려잡을 때는 저게 어미인가 싶다. 따지고 보면 수동 본인이 아내를 그렇게 잡아 버릇하니 그 분풀이가 아이에게로 가는지 모른다. 해도 저는 눈에 나게 맞을 짓을 하니까 매를 안 것이고, 이제 말이나 웅얼웅얼 뗀 아이 쪽은 무슨 용심으로 맷값을 사겠는가.

가령 아이를 잡을 때마다 아내는 꼭 '저 썩어 문드러

28

"When are you coming?" she'd wailed. "Geun-ho asks about you so often. It's not that easy to stay here."

"Why are you crying about this now? You're not staying at some stranger's house, right? I'll go as soon as I close the deal."

His wife was staying with her aunt on her mother's side who ran an inn in front of Suncheon Station. It must not have been too comfortable, though. An inn could be a rough place to stay. Besides, her aunt was an old woman, not so affectionate, perhaps, because she had been dealing with belligerent tramps all these years. At any rate, after today their suffering should be over. As soon as he sold his land off to the man from Naju, he was going to run away to Seoul or somewhere nearby. Su-dong was going to meet him at 11 a.m. Today, as a matter of fact.

Although Su-dong had found some of his wife's summer clothes, he could not find any long-sleeved clothes for this barmaid. *Petty! She must have taken everything she could.* Fortunately, a pair of baggy pants and a quilted jacket remained.

"Goodness! What are these for?"

Miss Jeong was surprised. She had probably ex-

질 종자들'이라는 욕지거리를 단다. 그것이 아이한테 하는 욕인가? 제 서방 들으라는 소리지. 해서 돌아서다가도 한 대 더 쥐어박게 된다. 아내의 지저분한 말기운은 아이 교육상에도 좋지 않다. 걸핏하면 고추 떨어진 딸내미로 안 태어나고 사내아이로 태어났느냐며 사내들을 원수로 삼으니 오죽하면 아이의 장래희망이 딸 되는 것이 되었을까. 그래서 친구놈들은 아이에게 장래희망 묻는 걸 즐겨한다.

"근호, 어른이 되면 뭐가 될 거지?"

그러면 아이는 제 어미를 훔쳐보며 "따알" 한다. 큼큼대는 친구놈들은 더 즐기느라고 아이의 고추를 낼름 훑어 먹는 시늉을 하며 짓궂게 "인자 근호 딸 됐네" 하였고, 철모르는 아이는 번번이 속으면서도 진짜인가 제 바지를 까뒤집어본다.

그래도 아이는 제 어미만 좋다고 졸졸 따를 뿐 아비 옆에는 얼씬도 않는다.

수동은 여자 머리에 챙이 넓은 모자까지 꾹 눌러준다.

"오히려 남들 눈에 더 띄지 않을까?"

모자를 살짝 잡아 빼 눈을 내놓으며 여자는 꺼림칙한 표정을 감추지 않는다. 말마따나 보자기에 대충 싼 것

pected him to take money out of the wardrobe. Instead, he pushed clothes that looked like they should have been sold at a flea market at her.

"Why advertise what happened last night? Just wear these!" Su-dong said.

"If I wear these I'll look even more ridiculous. Anyway, I don't have any reason to be embarrassed. I'm just getting out of work, you know."

"If they saw me, Jang Su-dong, having fun with you last night I'd probably be fine. But *you* won't be able to look the villagers straight in the eye when it's time for you to say good-bye."

"Thoughtful." She looked at him and seemed genuinely appreciative, but she continued putting on make-up while pushing the clothes away from her like they were a pile of old rags. After applying rouge around her pouting lips, she smacked them together without a care in the world.

"Goodness! Don't waste your energy! Why on earth are you putting make-up on when you're going to wear these clothes?" Su-dong, fretting openly now, took the rouge and powder case away from her and pushed them into her purse.

"No, I won't do it!" she turned to stare at Su-dong. "I ended up in this countryside to *not* wear

마냥 헐렁한 게 체대부터가 아내와는 멀다. 그것이야 집 나간 지 보름 만에 몸 고생 마음 고생에 시달리다 쪽 빠진 줄 미루어 짐작할 터이니 문제될 게 없다. 짐작이 안 된대도 단란주점 여자로만 알아주지 않으면 그만이다.

"아따! 누가 봐도 영락없이 내 여편네여."

하며 수동은 격려성으로 여자의 어깨를 툭 쳐주었다.

수동은 마당가에서 자전거를 끌고 나와 체인에 기름을 둘렀다. 여자가 뒷자리에 오르는데 무슨 영화 찍자는 속인지 한쪽으로 걸터앉아 발을 다소곳이 모은다. 수동은 가랑이를 쩍 벌리고 깊숙이 앉게 한다.

"허리를 꽉 보듬고 고개는 사정없이 수구려라이. 자, 그람 가드라고."

자전거는 내리막길을 내달리기 시작했다.

여자는 두 팔을 허리로 두르고 깍지 끼어 단단히 잡는다. 속도가 붙을수록 끙끙 앓는 소리가 나고 허리에 조여오는 힘이 더해진다. 종종 해보고 싶게 수동은 기분이 묘하다. 개 한 마리가 컹컹 짖으며 도랑을 건너 내뺀다. 웃배미 배밭에서 넉괭이자루 든 밀짚모자 하나가 일어선다. 김씨네들 선산 오르는 무렵에서 길은 완만하

clothes like theirs."

"After you slip out of this village, you can just throw them into a ditch or whatever."

"I'm saying I'm going to look like I just came out of a ditch right now if I wear these."

Although she became a little gentler, she still sat and sulked.

Su-dong pushed the pants into her arms. The pants had vines of either zucchini flowers or peonies printed on a maroon background. She shook the dust off the pants when she spread them, as if she was handling an old rag.

"Turn around."

"You're being ridiculous for someone who took off her underwear so casually..."

Su-dong opened the door a little and lit a cigarette. It seemed that a fishmonger had come to the village. A touting melody was rising and falling along the bend in the alley. The tune probably only sounded good to the person who was making it on the microphone. To others, there couldn't be any sound more aimless and meandering than that.

"Your lady must have been pretty big."

Miss Jeong turned around, grasping the waist of the baggy pants with her hands. They were so big

게 휘어지며 마을 가운데로 쭉 빠졌다.

동구 팽나무 정자가 눈앞의 목표점으로 달려든다. 돌연 가방 든 여자 하나가 그 그늘 아래서 비실비실 나온다. 한 손에는 아이가 달렸다. 수동은 급브레이크를 잡는다. 등허리에서 여자의 젖무덤이 물컹하게 뭉개진다.

"어이, 싸게 내려야 쓰겄다."

"왜에?"

여자가 뭉기적 뭉기적 내리며 묻는다. 정자 그늘을 빠져나온 여자와 아이는 진구네 담장 뒤로 사라진다. 자기 식구임에 분명하다. 머잖아 담장 그늘을 빠져나올 것이다.

수동은 자전거를 내던지고 여자의 등때기를 배밭으로 떠밀었다.

"저 선산 쪽으로 내빼라이."

"대체 누굴 봤는데 그래?"

"머리끄뎅이 안 뽑히고 싶으믄 싸게싸게 하랑께! 거 그까장 숨이 안 닿으믄 고 앞 마늘밭으로 꺼꾸러지고."

수동은 발을 동동 구른다. 이미 아내의 머리는 담장을 빠져나왔다. 남의 눈이 무서워 고개를 못 들고 걷길 망정이지 당장 이마만 세우면 못 볼 것을 보고 말리라.

that at least two bodies the size of Miss Jeong's could fit in them. Su-dong thought women were all about the same size, so he hadn't expected this. His wife had represented her high school as a shot putter. Her palms were as big as rice-cooker covers so he must have held them only a few times when he was wooing her. After that, he had treated them like they were feet.

When she hit their son with those hands, he doubted if she was fit to be a mother. But, perhaps, it was because Su-dong himself habitually beat his wife that she took it out on their son. Still, he beat her because she deserved it, but how on earth could a young child who had just begun to learn to speak deserve a beating?

For example, whenever Su-dong's wife beat their son, she would cry, "Son of a bunch of rotten bastards!" But how could she be directing a curse like that at a child? Clearly, it was directed at him. That was why he had to turn back around to smack her one more time. Her rough talk wasn't good for their son's education as well. She cursed him so much for being born male, crying why had he been born a boy, not a girl, a girl without that damn pepper, that their son eventually decided he want-

"얼렁!"

하며 수동이 허리를 꾸욱 찌르자 그제야 정양은 배밭으로 뛰어든다. 구두굽이 푹푹 빠졌다 나올 때마다 흙이 몇 점씩 찍혀 오른다. 바지가 흘러내리는지 고무줄 자리를 겨드랑이까지 끌어올린 채로다. 넥타이로라도 한번 둘러줄 것을……. 발놀림도 재고 낮은 가지 밑을 꿩 모양 잘도 빠져나간다. 어설퍼 보이긴 해도 한두 번 해본 실력이 아닌 듯싶다. 한하고 뛰어라! 옳지, 그짝으로 길을 잡아야 밭둑이 낮다! 속으로 응원을 하느라 수동은 절로 손이 불끈불끈 쥐어졌다.

"아빠!"

아이가 제 어미 손을 놓고 달려온다. 아내는 그 자리에 잠시 섰다. 염병할, 정양은 아직 마늘밭 둑도 못 올랐다. 선산까지는 어림없다. 바지를 엉덩이에 걸친 여자가 밭둑을 짚은 채 뒤돌아본다. 마늘밭으로 거꾸러지라고 수동이 날래게 턱짓을 했다.

수동은 자전거를 세워 받치고 괜히 무릎을 턴다.

달려드는 아이를 번쩍 안았다가 내려놓고 아내를 잡아먹을 듯 쏘아본다. 아내는 새들해져 눈알이 코끝에 걸렸다.

ed to become a daughter when he grew up. That was how bad it was. Su-dong's friends loved asking his son what he wanted to be when he grew up.

"Geun-ho, what do you want to be when you grow up?"

Su-dong's son would glance at his mother and say, "da-u-gh-ter." Then Su-dong's friends would continue to enjoy the scene themselves by pretending to pluck and eat the child's pepper and exclaim, "Geun-ho, now you're a girl!" Su-dong's son would stare wide-eyed down his own pants to see if it was true, even though they lied to him every time.

Still, their son always only followed his mom around. He never ventured near his dad.

Su-dong pushed a large-brimmed hat over Miss Jeong's head.

"Won't I stand out more wearing this?" Miss Jeong pushed the hat up a little above her eyes and shifted uncomfortably. As she had predicted, she looked completely unlike his wife. She looked like she had been haphazardly wrapped in kerchiefs. Still, people would assume that she had lost weight, had suffered mentally and physically for a

"도새 마음에 걸려싸서……."

기미가 부쩍 늘어 거뭇하게 뜬 낯으로 아내는 우물우물한다. 마음에 걸린다는 소리는 호필이를 위시한 동네 보증인들을 말할 것이다. 수동은 이를 악물고 손을 번쩍 치켜들었다. 움찔 눈을 감았지만 각오했다는 듯 아내는 뺨을 대놓고 섰다. 그 얼굴에서 생침 넘어가는 소리가 난다. 수동은 그 얼굴에 차마 손을 못 대고 스르르 무너진다.

"도시 안팎으로 손바닥이 맞어야제…… 암튼, 이따가 보자잉."

맵게 내뱉곤 곁눈질로 밭 쪽을 살피니 정양은 마늘밭에 등을 보인 채 앉았다. 딴에는 나물이라도 뜯는 시늉인지 어깨가 들먹거린다. 제 직업이 배우들 찜쪄먹는 직업이라고 자조 섞어 말을 하더니 헛말이 아니다.

"당신 참말로 뜰라고 맘 잡소?"

금세 아내는 살아났다. 수동은 대꾸하지 않는다.

"요새 도시들이 더 막막합디다. 비집고 들 틈자구가 없는 게 전쟁통보다 더하고."

제 이모 말일 것이다. 말대로 거기가 설령 전쟁통이라 해도 수동은 선택의 여지가 없다고 믿었다. 연대보증빚

fortnight after running away—so it wouldn't be too much of a problem. Even if they couldn't guess who she was, it would be okay as long as they didn't find out who she really was.

"Don't worry! Whoever sees you will think you're my wife." Su-dong patted her shoulders encouragingly.

Su-dong brought his bicycle from the edge of the yard to the front of his house and oiled its chains. Miss Jeong got on its back seat. She sat on its side and gathered her feet gently, as if she was being filmed. Su-dong made her straddle it securely.

"Hold on to me tight and lay your head low, as low as possible. Okay, let's go!"

The bicycle began to lurch down the slope.

Miss Jeong held onto his waist tightly, locking her fingers together. The faster he sped, the louder the moaning sound she made and the tighter her hands and arms gripped Su-dong's waist. It felt so oddly exciting that he wanted to do this again and again. A dog ran away across the brook, snapping and baying at them. A straw hat peeked up from a pear orchard above. The straw hat held a hoe. Around the entrance to the Kim family graveyard, the road

이 세 건이나 걸려서 이십여 호 마을을 통째로 들어먹게 생긴 마당이다. 한 건이야 이미 터졌고 두 건은 오늘 내일 한다. 돈을 똥으로 싸지르는 재주가 없는 이상 평생 빚쟁이를 벗어나지 못하게 생겼다. 당장 호필이 달려드는 것만 보아도 그렇다. 문대미골 저수지 우뜸 처삼촌 명의로 돌려둔 대지를 제 마음대로 처분해도 좋다는 각서를 받아가지 않았는가. 물론 호필이 걸려들어 잡혀먹은 재산이 그 가든 들어설 땅 값으로는 턱도 없다는 건 안다. 당장 제 배밭도 은행 앞으로 넘어가고 공공근로사업을 나다니니 트럭은 고사하고 마누라쟁이까지 내놓으래도 수동으로선 할 말이 없는 처지다. 용두리 양돈장 주인처럼 두루두루 송구스럽다는 유서를 남기고 농약병을 끌어 잡을 수 없는 바에야 차라리 평생 고향 땅을 못 밟는 죄인의 길을 선택하겠다는 것이다.

"저이는 누구까?"

아내가 마늘밭으로 고개를 틀고 섰다. 정양은 엉금엉금 두렁을 타고 넘어 밭 가운데에 앉아 있다. 저런 게 다 보이게 이제 아내는 여유가 도는 모양이다.

"누구긴 누구여? 김씨네 서울 메누리가 냉이 뜯는 모냥이지."

40

bent slowly and then veered straight into the village center.

A pavilion under a hackberry at the village entrance leapt up into the center of Su-dong's view. Suddenly, a woman holding a bag tottered out of the shade of the pavilion. She was holding a child with her other hand. Su-dong jammed the bike's brakes. He could feel Miss Jeong's breasts soft against his back.

"Hey. Get off. Now."

"Why?" Miss Jeong asked, leaping down.

The other woman and the child disappeared behind Jin-gu's house fence. They were clearly his wife and son. They would emerge from out of the shade of the fence fairly soon.

Su-dong threw his bicycle away and pushed Miss Jeong's back towards the pear orchard.

"Go to the family graveyard. Now," Su-dong ordered.

"Who the hell did you see?"

"If you don't want her to pull the hair out of your skull, get going. Quick! If you can't get to the graveyard, then lie low in the garlic field in front of it."

Su-dong was stamping his feet impatiently. His

41

"맨 비니루 깔린 마늘밭에서 뭔 냉이댜?"

"아따! 남이사 마늘밭에서 깨를 턴들……."

수동은 아내의 어깨를 집 쪽으로 돌려세운다. 마늘밭
으로 가는 눈길이 잦은 게 무슨 낌새를 챈 걸까? 수동은
아이의 조막손을 제 어미에게 잡혀주었다.

"어여 가 있어잉. 아빠 일 보고 후딱 갈 텡게. 자네는
가방 풀지 말고 있더라고. 남 속 뒤집는 일 좀 작작하고
앞으로 살 방도를 도모하란 말여."

수동은 서너 걸음이나 두 모자의 등을 떠밀고 올라갔
다. 두 모자가 정겹게 길을 오른다. 자전거에 올라선 그
는 다시 몸을 돌려서,

"행여 삼춘한테 전화 오믄 우정다방으로 오시라고 하
소. 인감도장 잊지 말고."

소리친다. 한시름 놓고 자전거를 굴린 수동이 "미안하
다이!" 하고 또 소리쳤는데 이번엔 돌아보는 여자가 두
여자였다. 그러나마나 자전거는 마을 가운데로 쏜살같
이 지나는 중이다.

도장을 누를 듯 누를 듯하다 만 게 벌써 한 시간째다.
이목구비가 똥그란 것이 의심 많게 생긴 인상이지만,
그만큼 침을 튀겼음에도 선뜻 도장을 못 박는 것은 너

wife's head was already visible above of the wall. She hadn't seen the two of them, she'd better have not, but only because she was lowering her head, avoiding eye contact with everyone passing by.

"Hurry!" Su-dong hissed.

Su-dong pushed Miss Jeong's waist hard in the direction of the graveyard. Only then did she leap into the pear orchard. Every time her heels dug deep into the earth, large divots of soil accompanied them out. It seemed her pants were falling down, because she was holding them up to her armpits by the elastic band. I should have offered her a necktie to wrap around her pants, Su-dong thought.

She was quick-footed and slipped under the low branches as skillfully as a pheasant. Although she looked somewhat clumsy, she was certainly a veteran when it came to running away. Get going! Su-dong thought. That's right, that's the way to get into the bank! Su-dong rooted for her silently. He clenched his fists without even being aware of it.

"Daddy!" Su-dong saw his son pluck his hand out of his mother's grip and ran towards him. His wife stood where their son left her. *Fuck!* Miss Jeong hadn't yet arrived at the garlic field embankment.

무 땅값이 헐해서 그런지 모른다. 좀 더 세게 부를 걸 그 랬나? 수동은 물을 들이켰다.

"저번에도 말씀드렸지만 여기저기 일 벌여논 게 많아 서 내불듯 내놓은 겁니다. 요새 으디 자금 만들기가 쉽 습니까? 보시다시피 근저당 설정된 것도 없이 아주 깨 끗한 땅이고요. 저도 가든 허가 내느라고 그 밑으로 돈 푼깨나 박았습니다."

권리금도 포기했다는 것을 알아달라는 뜻이다. 나주 사람은 고개를 주억거리면서도 줄곧 주무르고 있던 부 동산 등기부를 또 뒤적거리고 든다.

"거야 우리 조카사위 말이 틀림읎제. 에또……."

처삼촌이 거든다. 커피만 마시다가 일어나라고 단단 히 주의시켰건만 지켜보는 본인도 무척 답답했던 모양 이다. 아까는 연신 하품을 해대기에 커피를 한 잔 더 시 켜 드시랬더니 밤에 통 잠이 안 온다고 손사래를 쳤다.

"은행 한 번 안 댕게온 문서요. 갱치가 좋아서 식당만 채러노믄 차 있는 놈들이 대구 몰리리다. 암, 그 근방이 근동에선 젤루다 볼 만허지. 에또, 아모리 가물어도 거 그 저수지는 물이 보트지럴 안 해."

하고 말에 불이 붙는 것을 수동은 허벅지를 지그시 눌

She had a long way to go to get the Kim family graveyard. Her pants hung loosely down her rear, and she turned back towards Su-dong, resting her hand on the embankment as she did so. Su-dong nodded quickly to the garlic field, trying to convey that she should fall flat.

Su-dong stood his bicycle up and snapped out the kickstand while he dusted his knees.

His son crashed into Su-dong's arms and Su-dong swept him up high into the air before putting him down. Then, he stared at his wife hard as if he was about to swallow her whole. Standing right under his nose, his wife seemed to shrink like a cabbage wilting in the heat.

"I felt so guilty..." she said. Her face darkened and Su-dong could see her freckles and lines of worry spread across her face. She probably meant that she felt guilty towards all the co-signers in the village like Ho-pil. Su-dong clenched his teeth and raised his hand up at her. Although his wife flinched and closed her eyes, she actually leaned toward him, as if expecting it. He could hear her swallow hard. Su-dong couldn't hit that face. He melted right before her.

"Well, we need two hands to clap, don't we?

러 껐다. 틀린 말은 아니지만 이구동성으로 밀어붙이면 오히려 역효과만 난다. 문서상 아무 하자가 없는 땅을 두고 여러 말이 필요 없다. 실제로 수동이 가든을 지을 작정으로 은행돈을 끌어다가 마련한 땅이다. 금점판이 성했던 골짜기라 지금은 비록 오두막들은 헐리고 없지만 버젓이 대지로 살아 있는 땅이었다. 그리고 가든에 단란주점 허가까지 따냈다. 문제는 동네사람들이었다. 개를 잡네, 돼지고기를 굽네 해서 구워삶을 때는 다들 파리떼 꼬이듯 하더니 건설 자재를 옮겨놓자 진정서니 연판장이니 하는 것들을 돌려 발목을 잡았다. 그뿐인가. 행정심판 뒤에는 꽹과리까지 두드리며 길을 막아 굴삭기가 아예 범접도 못했다. 아무리 좋아진 세상이라지만 남의 사유재산을 두고 감 놔라 배 놔라 하는 처사는 무엇인가. 이런 게 민주화라면 세상이 영 틀리게 돌아가는 것이다. 저수지 농업용수가 오염된다는 게 마을사람들 주장인데, 본심은 제 남정네고 여편네가 오염될까 지레 걱정이 된 데 있을 거다. 또 모른다. 지지리 가난한 집 자손이 잘되는 꼴을 못 봐서 그럴는지도. 아무튼 그 땅엔 이 장수동이 아니라 대통령이 들어와도 벽돌 한 장 못 놓게끔 일이 돌아가 있었다.

Anyway, let's talk later. Got it?" Su-dong looked back out towards the garlic field. Miss Jeong was still sitting out there, facing the other direction. She must have been pretending that she was picking wild greens; he could see her shoulders clearly going up and down. She often said self-deprecatingly that her profession required more acting than an actual acting job. Su-dong didn't think she'd really been joking.

"Are you really planning to run away?" his wife said, energized by Su-dong's change in attitude.

Su-dong didn't respond.

"It's even harder in cities these days. There's no room for outsiders to squeeze their way in. It's worse than it was during the war," she continued.

That must have been what her aunt had said to her. But, Su-dong felt that he had no choice but to run away, even if he literally had to end up in battle. He was about to bankrupt this entire village of about twenty families because of three of his debts and because the villagers had been his co-signers. One debt had already burst, and the other two would in a day or two. Unless he had the magical ability to shit money, he would have to live his entire life crushed under the weight of unbearable

"당장 경제가 풀리면 그냥 넘겨도 몇 장은 너끈히 불려줄 땅입죠."

해놓고 수동은 한마디 더 보탰다.

"박 사장님! 문의전화가 쇄도를 합니다."

드디어 작자가 돋보기를 벗는다.

"나야 더 볼 것 없이 좋지만 밑에 동생들도 한번 둘러봤으면 싶어 하는 눈치라……. 그리고 땅 매매란 게 쓰고 버리는 물건 거래완 달라 자꾸 신중해집니다."

제법 점잖다.

"하믄요!"

처삼촌이 맞장구를 치고 든다. 수동은 속으로 끙, 했다. 동생 운운하며 드는 작자의 꾐수가 훤히 보인다. 지레 겁을 줘서 저를 속일 생각은 말라는 뜻일 게다. 누구를 촌것으로 아나. 수동이 진작에 밑천 삼아 골백번도 더 써먹어본 수작이다.

"아무튼 한 번 더 둘러보고 계약해도 실례가 안 되겠지요?"

나주 사람이 자리를 털고 일어난다. 물어놓고 대답은 안 챙기는 버르장머리는 또 뭔가.

"허허, 땅이 어디 갔을라구요?"

debts. He just had to think of what Ho-pil had forced him to do. Hadn't he gotten a memorandum from Su-dong guaranteeing that Ho-pil could do whatever he wanted with Su-dong's land above the Mundaemigol Reservoir, the land nominally owned by Su-dong's wife's uncle?

Su-dong knew, of course, that Ho-pil could not even come close to paying off the assets he had lost because of Su-dong with the money he would get for the land Su-dong had planned to build a luxury restaurant on. Ho-pil had lost his pear or-chard to the bank and worked as a day laborer at public works sites, so there was nothing Su-dong could complain about. Even if Ho-pil demanded something like his truck—or even his wife. He couldn't pluck an agrichemical bottle from off the ground, as a pig farmer in Yongdu-ri had done, and write a will that said he was sincerely sorry to everyone; Su-dong had no choice but to choose a criminal's road, one he could never come back from.

"Who's that over there?" His wife was looking off in the direction of the garlic field. Miss Jeong crawled over the embankment slowly and sat in the middle of the field. Su-dong's wife must have re-

하고 수동은 맥없이 따라 일어섰다. 나주 사람은 이미 다방 문을 나서고 있다.

"또 오세요!"

나주 사람한테는 허리가 꺾어진 종업원이 수동이 가슴 앞으로는 손바닥을 내민다. 수동은 검지에 침을 발라 허공으로 찍 그었다. 김양은 대번에 무슨 썩은 것 씹은 표정으로 변한다.

"오빠? 가끔 한 번씩은 정리를 해줘야죠."

"아따, 적금 드는 셈 쳐라. 그래 내 일수 찍데끼 날마다 안 들르디? 두고 봐라마는 잔으로 나간 돈이 바가지로 들어올 테니. 미쓰 김아, 으디 나도 한번 또 오세욜 들어보자, 잉?"

"그게 아무한테나 나오나 뭐. 외상만 갚아봐요. 화장실 갈 때도 해주지."

김양은 통통 부어서 돌아선다. 수동은 엉덩이를 툭 쳐주고 다방을 나섰다. 언제 들었는지 그의 입엔 이쑤시개가 꽂혀 있다.

문대미골 저수지를 끼고 도는 길엔 산벚꽃이 한창이다. 물비린내인지 흙내인지 쿠더분한 냄새가 코끝에 감긴다. 물오른 버들은 늘어져 살랑살랑 머리를 감고, 그

gained her calm completely if she could notice something like that.

"Who else could it be? Mr. Kim's daughter-in-law from Seoul must be picking a pick-purse."

"A pick-purse covered in plastic?"

"Why do you even care? What would it matter if she was even shaking sesame in a garlic field?"

Su-dong held his wife by the shoulders and turned her around towards the direction of his house. But his wife kept looking out to the garlic field. Did she suspect something? Su-dong took his son's tiny hand and brought it to his wife's.

"Go home, okay? Daddy will take care of his business and come back soon. You shouldn't unpack. Please don't do anything that upsets me any more. Let's find a way to get through this!"

Su-dong walked with his wife and son a few steps, giving them a few gentle nudges in the direction of their house. Mother and son walked up the slope, holding hands affectionately. After getting back on his bicycle, Su-dong turned around again and yelled, "If your uncle calls, tell him to come to Ujeong Tea House. And don't forget his registered seal."

A little relieved, Su-dong rode his bicycle a while

깊은 그늘 아래서 끼룩끼룩 비오리 노는 소리 들린다. 나주 사람이 저수지에 눈길을 주느라 승용차는 자못 느리게 비포장길을 밟는다. 옴팡하여 한갓지고 볕드는 곳이면 어김없이 낚시꾼이 들어앉아 있다. 이태 전 저수지 물을 방류한 뒤로는 물고기 입질이 시원찮은데도 시절 탓인지 낚시꾼은 더 늘었다.

갈잎 부리고 늦잠 든 문대미 산그림자가 알몸으로 차앞 덮개 위에 미끄러진다. 아무래도 수동은 저 쇠불알처럼 헐벗은 산을 손님에게 보이고 싶지 않다.

"삼동 내내 없어 보이는 산일수록 여름이 좋은 법이지요."

제법 그럴듯하게 둘러댔다 싶다. 너른 공터가 있는 큰 문대미가 시야에 들어온다.

"나까지 갈 필요 없겠지라? 나넌 여그서 바람이나 쐬고 있을 텡게 후딱 댕게오씨요. 오래 기다리게 하지 맙시다."

수동은 차에서 내린다. 실은 공터에서 쓰레기 포대를 들고 얼쩡거리는 호필을 목격한 것이다. 놈에게 덜미가 잡히면 사문서 위조고 뭐고 덮어놓고 물에 처박으려 들게다. 미안한 마음이 전혀 없는 바도 아니다. 하나, 친구

and turned around again to yell, "I'm sorry!" This time, two women turned around. No matter, his bicycle was passing quickly through the village center.

It had been already an hour since he had had to get his seal stamped. The man from Naju had a roundish face, and so he looked like he would be suspicious. But it might have been because the price of the land was so cheap that he couldn't finish the deal despite Su-dong's eloquence. Should I have asked for more? Su-dong thought. Su-dong took a sip of water.

"As I said before, I just have too many projects going on and so I'm practically giving this property away. I know it's not easy to come up with a large sum these days. As you can see, I haven't even used this land as collateral. It's clean land. I had to spend a considerable sum to get the restaurant permit, too."

Su-dong meant that he had given up his premium. Although the Naju businessman was nodding his head, he tried again to take a close look at the real estate register.

"What my nephew-in-law said is exactly right. Anyway..." His wife's uncle interjected. Although

좋다는 것도 어려운 일 당해봐야 안다. 적으나마 된 친구라면 각서를 받거나 트럭을 압수하지는 않는다. 놈이 돌쩌귀를 뽑았으니 나는 들보인들 못 들어낼까.

"욕보시네."

수동은 성끗 웃어놓고 본다. 찔레덩굴 틈에서 집게로 신문지를 들어내던 호필이 고개를 쳐든다. 아직 술때를 못 씻어 푸석한 얼굴이다.

"왜 왔어?"

노상 그 툽상스런 인사다.

"몸살나고 싶어 왔지."

"남 파트너 훔쳐가더니 거기선 몸살 안 나고 왜 여기서 찾어?"

"글쎄 말일세. 아침에 눈 떠보고 자네한테 또 한 번 감격은 했네만."

수동은 쭈그려 앉아 담배에 불을 붙인다. 호필에게 한 개비 내밀자,

"방금 했네."

하곤 그도 옆에 앉는다. 볕이 좋아 절로 소매가 중중 올라간다.

"저수지 괴기 씨가 마르겠어. 주말이고 주중이고 가지

Su-dong had told him to just sit back and have some coffee until the deal was finished, he must have become anxious, too. He kept on yawning and Su-dong offered to order more coffee. But he waved his hand away, saying he wouldn't be able to fall asleep at night if he drank any more.

"That register has never even been to the bank. The view here is beautiful. As soon as you set up a restaurant here rich people will just swarm to it. Of course, this land has the most beautiful view in the area. By the way, the water in the reservoir never dries out even when there's a drought." His wife's uncle was rambling now.

Su-dong, however, put out the fire by gently kneeing him in his thigh. Although what he had said was indeed true, an overly eager push from two people could have the opposite effect. You didn't have to list the merits of the land over and over again when the property came with clean documentation. In fact, Su-dong had bought it to build a luxury restaurant on himself, borrowing money from several banks in order to do so. Since the valley used to be a goldmine site, it still remained as a building site even after the old huts had been demolished. Su-dong had actually been

덜을 않고 아예 텐트를 치고 주저앉았겄네. 쓰레기가 말도 못혀."

호필이 맞은편 솔숲 자리의 낚시꾼을 건너다보며 말한다.

"냅둬. 을매나 속들이 상혔겄어. 그리고 은제 우리가 저 물꾀기 묵고 살았능가? 쓰레기도 자꾸 내부러야 공공근로도 안 떨어질 테구."

"쓰레기가 보통으루 많아야 말이제. 저그 문대미골 골짝으로는 경운기 하나를 채우고도 다 못 실어내 쌓아뒀네."

올라간 차는 아직 보이지 않는다. 수동은 담배를 비벼 껐다.

"호필이!"

수동은 불러놓고, 그쪽이 돌아앉자 잠시 뜸을 들였다가

"트럭 키 좀 주게. 집사람을 데꼬 와야 쓰겄어."

한다.

"찾었남?"

목소리를 은근히 깔고 드는 게 외려 수동이 낯뜨겁다.

"으응. 순천 지 이모네에 있다는구만."

able to get permission for not only the luxury res-taurant but also a hostess bar.

The problem with his whole plan was with the villagers. The villagers, the same villagers who'd swarmed his land like flies when Su-dong offered them free meals with dog meat soup and bar-bequed pork, blocked his way and circulated peti-tions once Su-dong began to bring in building ma-terials. Not only that, but they'd also blocked the road, beating gongs and whatnot, after the admini-strative decision, so the excavator hadn't been able to even get near the site.

No matter if the world was generally a better place to live in, how could they demand this and that about someone else's private property? If this was democracy, something still was definitely wrong with the world.

The villagers claimed that the farming water in the reservoir would be contaminated, but what ac-tually worried them was the contamination of their spouses. Besides, they probably couldn't tolerate the thought of some son of dirt-poor family lin-eage making it big. Anyway, the situation now was that not only Jang Su-dong, but also even the president of the country couldn't lay a single brick

"하, 잘된 일이네! 암튼 바람나서 한 짓이 아닝께 막 몰진 말라고."

호필은 허리춤에서 열쇠고리를 풀어낸다. 별일이다. 제 마누라도 돌아오는 듯이 호들갑이라니······. 어쩌면 제 딴에는 한시름 놓았는지도 모른다. 마누라가 가출을 했으니 이곳에 더 미련 없는 그 바깥놈이 언제 뜰지 모른다 싶었을 테고, 해서 부랴부랴 트럭부터 잡고 들었을 게다. 이럴 줄 알았으면 진작에 써볼 일이었다.

"고맙네."

수동은 열쇠를 받으며 시늉으로라도 고개를 주억거린다.

"면에서 사람 나올 때가 돼서 나는 올라가봐야 쓰겠네. 이따 밤에 한번 들름세. 아 참······."

호필은 돌아서서 포대 끈에 묶어둔 웬 주먹만한 물건을 풀어낸다. 난데없는 새다. 날개가 묶여 눈만 뒤룩거리는 놈은 산비둘기보다 약간 작은 몸집이다. 부리가 매처럼 날카롭고 머리와 가슴은 온통 황갈색이다.

"풀새밭에 박힌 것을 잡았네. 근호 녀석이 좋아하겠제? 헤헤."

새를 건네받을 때 놈은 '히이요' 하는 소리를 내며 운

there.

"As soon as the economy gets better, you can make a few bucks just by flipping it," Su-dong said, "President Park! I've actually been flooded with calls inquiring about the property."

Finally, the man from Naju removed his reading glasses.

"I like it so much that I don't even think I have to look at it again. But my brothers, on the other hand, insist that I take a second look... Land transaction, after all, is a different sort of matter than dealing with things that you would simply use and throw away. So I do feel I have to be prudent."

He was quite the gentleman.

"Of course!" Su-dong's uncle-in-law agreed readily.

Su-dong's heart sank. He recognized immediately what the man from Naju was contriving to do by mentioning his brothers: he was threatening Su-dong. In effect, he was trying to convey to Su-dong that he wouldn't be able to fool him without consequences.

He thinks I'm a country bumpkin, huh! Su-dong thought. Su-dong himself had used that kind of trick more than a hundred times.

다. 손등을 콕 찍는 게 성깔이 보통이 아니다.

"매 그짝 종자인감?"

"그렇다."

"자네 딸내미한테나 주제 그랑가?"

"그 애린 것이 처신을 한당가."

수동은 호필이 얼굴을 다시 한 번 쳐다본다. 겪어보지
만 철없는 애들 같은 구석이 많다.

"이따 늦을지 모르니께 천천히 올라오소. 맹색이 조카
사위가 그런 일로 찾어가서 저녁밥도 안 뜨고 일어서기
도 그렇고……."

"하믄! 암튼 백 번 참어서 잘 달레 뫼셔와. 나가 봐도
자넨 각시 없으믄 완전히 베러부러."

호필이 당부하다시피 해놓고 골짜기 쪽으로 사라진
다. 수동은 새를 들여다본다. 그렇게 봐서 그런지 몰라
도 놈의 검고 작은 눈빛이 애처로워 보인다. 하늘에서
는 어땠는지 몰라도 이렇듯 날개가 묶였으니 놈도 천상
참새나 비둘기 그것들과 다를 게 없는 순한 새일 따름
이다.

"니도 잘나가는 시절 다 가부렀다잉? 날 보그라. 니하
고 다를 게 하나도 읎어야. 인자 살어갈 날개는 읎고 도

"At any rate, I hope I'm not acting impolitely if I look around one more time before I stamp my seal. Would that be okay?"

With that, the man from Naju rose. How polite is it to ask a question but not wait for an answer? The man wasn't quite as genteel as he looked.

"Well, the land's not just going to get up and run away," Su-dong said and tried to laugh heartily. He rose helplessly along with him.

The man from Naju was already opening the tea-shop door and was making his way outside.

"Please come again, sir!"

After bowing low to the man from Naju, the wait-ress thrust her palm towards Su-dong's chest. Su-dong wet his forefinger and drew a line in the air. Miss Kim's expression immediately turned rotten.

"Hey, brother! You have to pay your tab at least every once in a while."

"Yeesh. Just consider it your savings," Su-dong waved her off. "Haven't I come here everyday as if I were making a daily deposit? Wait and see! The money that's been going out by the cup will return by the gourd. Miss Kim, let's hear a 'Please come again, sir!' next time. All right?"

"Those words don't just come out of my mouth

망갈 날개만 남어부렀응께……."

수동은 중얼거리며 되게 묶인 노끈을 느슨하게 풀어 날개가 좀 놀 수 있게 해준다. 새 부리에 손끝을 대본다. 그러자 놈이 콕 쪼고 든다.

담배 한 대 참이나 지나 나주 사람 차가 문대미골에서 내려왔다.

마음을 굳혔으리라. 마음이 다급해진 수동은 차가 서기 무섭게 문고리부터 당긴다. 작자의 낯빛은 기대했던 것보다 시원찮다. 요게 또 왜 이러시나? 입술이 다 말려들게 입을 꾹 다물고 있다.

"장사장, 혹 땅 문제로 민원 같은 것 있습니까?"

"왜, 누가 뭐랍디까?"

수동이 덤빌 듯 묻는다. 나주 사람은 뒷좌석으로 손을 뻗어 천 무더기를 뒤집어 보인다. 걸레짝 같은 현수막이다. 저거구나! 지난해 여름에 걷어다가 골짜기 방공호 속에 처박아버린 것들 중 하나임에 틀림없는데 저것을 무슨 수로 찾아 짊어지고 왔나 싶다. 부러 찾으려 해도 찾기 힘든 것들이다.

"이게 쓰레기 더미에 있잖소. 가든건설 결사반대. 이건 또 뭐야? 동네에서 내걸은 모양이군. 암튼 이런 게

62

for anyone. Pay up! I'll remind you even when you're on your way to the bathroom."

Miss Kim turned around sullenly. Su-dong gave her a single gentle pat on her rear and got up. He snapped a toothpick into his mouth, which he must have picked up on his way out.

Wild cherries were blooming along the road around the Mundaemigol Reservoir. A stuffy smell —perhaps from the water or maybe the soil—lingered in everyone's nose. Weeping willows were washing their hair in the water and the playful honking of geese sounded out from under their shade. The man from Naju was looking out at the reservoir and so their car advanced rather slowly along the unpaved road. Wherever it was secluded and sunny, there were anglers. Since the reservoir water had been discharged two years ago, the fish didn't bite as much as they had before. There were more anglers here now, perhaps because of the hard times.

The shadow of the naked Mundaemi hill, sleeping in late after shedding all its leaves last fall, glided over the hood of the car. If possible, Su-dong would have not shown the mountain, as naked and ugly as a pair of ox testicles, to his guest.

저 위에 한둘이 아니요."

넨장, 공공근로사업 나온 품꾼들이 끄집어다가 그러모아 놓은 모양이다. 대충 눈에 띄는 쓰레기나 치울 일이지 무슨 대단한 밥벌이줄이라고 꽁꽁 감추어둔 것까지 죄 끌어 내놓았느냔 말이다.

"아, 그거요잉? 하하, 한때 오해가 좀 있어부렀지요. 다 끝난 문젠디……."

"무슨 오햅니까?"

작자는 몰아치듯 묻는다.

"그건 뭐 벨 건 아니고라…… 여그가 도립공원으로 묶인다는 맹랑한 소문이 돌았제요. 그람 건 뭔 소리겄어요? 당장 땅값이 못 쓰게 된다 이거지요잉. 그래 동네가 쬐끔 시끄러웠습죠. 그땐 나도 앞장섰지만서두…… 곧 근거 없는 소문으로 드러나 싱겁게 끝나부렀습니다."

수동은 이마에서 땀을 찍어냈다. 불에 처지르지 않고 박아놓은 것이 후회스럽다.

"눈으로 본 이상 좀 더 두고 봐야겠소."

나주 사람은 차창을 올려버린다. 이내 차는 먼지를 일으키며 미끄러져 간다.

수동은 차가 방죽 너머로 사라질 때까지 황망히 서

"The more naked a mountain looks during the three months of winter, the better it is in summer," Su-dong said.

He felt he had managed the situation pretty decently. The big Mundaemi with its large glade came into his view.

"You don't need me there, do you? I'll take the air here. Please look around and come back quickly. Please don't make me wait too long."

Su-dong got out of the car. The fact was that he had just seen Ho-pil lingering in the glade, trash sack in hand. If Ho-pil caught him selling the land, he would simply dump Su-dong into the water. Next, he would even be accused of forging a private document. Of course, Su-dong felt sorry for Ho-pil. But, a friend in need was a friend in deed, as they said. If he were a real friend, Ho-pil would not have demanded a memorandum from Su-dong or have confiscated Su-dong's truck. If Ho-pil had taken off the hinges, why shouldn't he remove the crossbeam?

"You're pushing yourself too hard," Su-dong said, and smiled at him. Ho-pil, who had been picking up a newspaper that had gotten stuck in a brier vine, looked up. His face looked swollen and

있었다. 손아귀를 얼마나 불끈거렸는지 히이요, 새가 다 운다.

터덜터덜 집으로 들어서자 아이는 토방에 앉아 흙장난질이고 아내는 보이지 않는다.

"옛다! 도망 안 가게 잘 보듬고 놀아라이."

수동은 아이에게 새를 건네준다. 처음에는 무서워하는 눈치더니 아빠가 깃을 한 번 쓰다듬어주자 아이는 이내 조막손을 내민다.

"근호, 아빠랑 엄마랑 서울 가고 싶쟈?"

"응."

"그람 으디 가지 말고 이 새 갖고 집에서 놀아야쓴다이."

"으응."

수동은 아이의 볼을 토닥여주고 집 안을 둘러본다. 안사람 든 흔적이라곤 없이 마루에 걸레짝은 던져진 채 말라 있고, 또 그 한구석에 열흘 동안 벗어놓은 빨래가 뭉쳐 있다. 빗자루질 탄 지 오래인 빗도랑에선 지렁이라도 근실근실 기어나올 것 같다.

"엄마는?"

"……"

새를 가지고 노느라 아이는 기척도 없다. 토방에 놓인

hung-over.

"Why are you here?" As usual, his greeting was blunt.

"I came to get sick."

"You stole someone else's partner, so why not get sick there?"

"That's right. I opened my eyes this morning and I was touched. Truly honestly touched. Giving up the girl for me."

Su-dong squatted and lit his cigarette. When Su-dong offered one to Ho-pil, he said, "I just smoked one." Ho-pil sat beside Su-dong. The sun was so warm they ended up rolling up their sleeves without even thinking about it.

"The fish in the reservoir are all going to die off. Those anglers don't leave during the weekdays or the weekends. They'll end up pitching tents and living here. So much trash!" Ho-pil stared out at an angler near the pine grove.

"Let them be. They must be hurting to have to fish here. Anyway, when did we ever have to live on the fish here? The more trash they throw away, the more public works there'll be."

"The amount of trash they leave here is just enormous, though. Even after taking a lot of them

신발로 보아 아내는 방에 드러누운 모양이다. 세월 좋다. 정작 드러누워야 할 당사자는 밖에 세워두고 내다보지도 않는다. 오랜만에 집구석이라고 들었으면 마루도 훔치고 냉장고에서 뭐가 썩고 있는지 들여다봐야 도리 아닌가. 수동은 부아가 나서 신발을 털어 벗고 방문을 획 당겼다.

대번에 얼굴에 날아드는 것이 있다. 코쭝배기를 간질이고 떨어지는 것은 도넛처럼 뭉킨 검은 망사 스타킹이다. 칠칠치 못한 년, 이걸 다 벗어놓고 갈 게 뭐람. 채 정신을 수습 못하고 섰는데, 또 날아드는 건 붉은 루주 묻은 화장지다.

"요 짓거리 하느라고 애새끼랑 내돌렸냐?"

아내는 가방 옆에 입은 채로 퍼질러 앉아 악다구니다. 수동은 문턱 앞에 엎드려 이 경을 치르니 우선 아이에게 부끄럽다.

"……뭣도 모르고 너 시방 왜 이라냐? 호필이한테 방을 빌려줬다니께. 워매, 환장하겠네이!"

"호필이 호필이…… 그래 이 썩어 문드러질 종자야, 마늘밭에서 깨도 털드라. 네이, 니가 그래도 살을 둘러쓴 짐승이라믄……."

away in a cultivator there was still a huge pile of left-over trash in Mundaemigol Valley."

The car hadn't come back yet. Su-dong put out his cigarette.

"Ho-pil!"

Ho-pil took a while to turn around, but when he did Su-dong asked him, "Please give me my truck keys back. I have to bring my wife back."

"You found her?" The way Ho-pil lowered his voice made Su-dong's face burn.

"Yes. I heard that she's staying with her aunt in Suncheon."

"Hey, that's a great news!" Ho-pil gave him a genuine smile. "Well, since she didn't run away with a lover, don't push her too hard." Ho-pil took the key ring out from around his waist.

Ridiculous! He was acting as if his own wife was coming back. Perhaps, he was relieved. He must have thought that Su-dong was liable to run away at any time since even his wife had left him. That must have been why Ho-pil had hurried to confiscate Su-dong's truck keys. If Su-dong had known Ho-pil had felt this way, he would have tried this trick earlier.

"Thank you," Su-dong said, taking the key and

또 이러며 날아드는 게 요번엔 그중 작다. 꼬깃꼬깃 뭉친 종잇조각이다. 오랫동안 쥐고 있었는지 땀에 젖었다. 펼쳐보니 단란주점 영수증. 어이쿠! 결국 그년이 마누라를 상대했구나.

"사업상으로다……."

하다 말고 수동은 아내가 재떨이를 쥐어 드는 것을 보고 날래게 문을 닫았다. 다행히 재떨이는 날아오지 않는다. 그는 토방 아래로 내려서며,

"그래서 돈을 줬냐?"

물었고, 안에서는

"미쳤어! 거기 내줄 돈 두고 시방 우리가 이 용천이야?"

하는 대답이 나온다. 정양 안부는 물으나 마나다. 서방한테 해대는 게 저 정도니 부실한 그쪽은 아마 몸 한 축이 절단이 나도 단단히 났으리라. 또 모른다. 그쪽도 작심하고 마누라를 상대한 눈치니 고발이네 어쩌네 해싸며 서방 단속까지 충고해주고 돌아갔을 테고, 빚하고 법 소리만 들어도 쏙 주눅이 드는 아내는 납죽 배웅까지 했는지.

수동은 변소로 가 앉는다. 주머니에서 담뱃갑을 빼 들

pretending to nod his head in gratitude.

"I have to go back now. It's about time for the *my-eon* official to show up. I'll drop by later tonight. Oh, by the way..."

Ho-pil turned around, untied the sack he was holding, and removed something the size of a fist from it. Of all things, it was a bird. It was a bit smaller than a turtledove and its wings were tied back. It looked around with wide, bulbous eyes. Its beak was as sharp as a hawk's and its head and breast were yellowish brown.

"I caught it from the grass field where it got stuck. Geun-ho will like it, won't he?" Ho-pil laughed.

As Ho-pil handed it to Su-dong the bird cried, "Hyiyo." Immediately, it pecked the back of Su-dong's hand; it must have had quite the temper.

"Looks some kind of hawk, right?"

"I heard it might be."

"Why don't you give it to your daughter?"

"You don't think she's a bit too young to take care of it?"

Su-dong looked at Ho-pil's face again. The more he got to know him, the more he realized that Ho-pil had quite a childlike innocence about him.

었으나 빈껍데기뿐이다.

"니 애비놈은 어디 가던?"

"모야."

아내가 마루로 나오는 기척이다. 수동은 밑으로 부엌
부엌 새는 소리를 조여 막는다.

아내의 땅 꺼지는 한숨소리가 들린다.

"엄마, 요거 이름이 모야?"

"몰러! 니 잘난 애비한테 물어봐라. 지금 새타령이 나
오게 생겼냐? 에그, 이 썩어 문드러질 종자야!"

종주먹으로라도 쥐어박았는지 아이가 울먹인다. 저
런 못난 년! 자식을 아주 버려놓고 있다.

"그만 뚝! 뭐긴 뭐겠냐? 자지 물어갈 새제."

저 말하는 꼬라지 좀 봐라. 수동은 끙 일어났다 앉는다.

"자지물어갈새?"

아이는 눈물 밴 목소리로 되뇌어본다.

아내는 부엌으로 들어가고 수동은 그 틈을 노려 안방
으로 기어든다. 그는 가방을 베개로 삼아 벌렁 드러누
웠다. 종일 시달린 몸도 몸이지만 오늘밤으로 서울까지
밟으려면 좀 자둬야겠어서다.

얼마나 눈을 붙였을까. 돌연 밖에서 아이의 자지러지

"I might be late this evening, so can you please drop by a little later than usual? I can't visit my wife's aunt and come back without having dinner with her, especially for matters like these, you know how it goes..."

"Of course!" Ho-pil said. "Anyway, just try to be really patient with her. Take it easy on her and bring her back by being respectful. You're a mess without your wife, y'know. I can tell."

Ho-pil continued to practically beg Su-dong to take it easy on his wife as he made way in the direction of the valley and out of sight. After he left, Su-dong looked down at the bird. Probably because of how he felt at the moment, the bird's eyes looked pathetic to Su-dong. No matter what it was like for the bird when it had been high in the sky, it was now docile, its wings tied, no different than a sparrow or a dove.

"The good old days are all gone for you too, huh?" Su-dong muttered. "Look at me. I'm not all that different from you. I don't have wings to fly with or live on, just wings for running away..." Su-dong loosened the rope a little, so the bird could move its wings a little bit. Then, Su-dong put his fingertip onto the tip of its beak. The bird pecked

는 울음소리가 들린다. 아내가 후닥닥 부엌에서 뛰어나와 버럭 고함을 친다. 저런 원수 같은 것들! 수동은 몸을 뒤챈다. 이럴 땐 혼자 사느니만 못하다. 이젠 아내를 좀 잡아줘야겠다는 생각에 수동은 천근같은 몸을 끌어 문고리를 잡았다.

아이는 토방에 앉아 울고 있는데 아랫도리를 반이나 드러낸 채다. 아마 빗도랑에 오줌이라도 누다가 그만 새를 놓치고 저러는가 싶다. 아이의 손에도 제 어미의 손에도 새는 보이지 않는다.

바지를 내려뜨린 아이는 제 어미를 올려다보며,

"깨물어만 보고 기양 가부렀다."

하고 울먹이는데, 그만 사색이 된 아내는 누가 고추를 훔쳐 갈세라 아이의 바지를 홀떡 추켜올려주며,

"워매, 썩을 놈! 뭔 지랄한다고 고것을 새한테 내보이냐!"

하는 거다. 아이의 사정도 못 헤아리는 깜깜한 아내는 또 아이를 잡아대기 시작한다. 절로 담배가 당긴 수동은 꽁초 수북한 재떨이를 끌어당겼다.

『매향』, 실천문학사, 1999

at it.

In about the time it took for Su-dong to finish a cigarette, the man from Naju's car came down from Mundaemigol.

He must have made up his mind by now. Feeling impatient, Su-dong pulled the car door open as soon as the car came to a rest. The man's face did not look as pleased as Su-dong expected. What was the matter with him now? His mouth was closed so tight that his lips almost rolled inward.

"President Jang, have there been any public grievances about the land?"

"Why do you ask? Has somebody said something?" Su-dong was aggressive.

The man from Naju stretched his arm to the back seat of his car and fumbled at a heap of fabric in the back. He pulled out a tattered placard. *Goodness!* It was one of the signs he had taken down last summer and thrown away into an air-raid shelter in the valley. Su-dong wondered how on earth he could have found it and carried it back with him. It would have been hard to find even for someone who was intentionally looking for it.

"I found this on top of a pile of garbage: Absolutely No Restaurant!" the man read.

"And look at this!" he brandished the sign at Su-dong. "The villagers must have hung it. And there were a lot of these over there, too."

Fuck! The day laborers at the public works must have taken them all out and piled them together. Why on earth had they taken all the trash out from a hiding place like that instead of just cleaning up what had been clearly lying there? Working as if this clean-up job was something they were proud of, that actually provided for their livelihood.

"Oh, that?" Su-dong tried to laugh. "That was just a misunderstanding. It's all over now."

"What was the misunderstanding?" the man raised his eyebrows.

"It was nothing, really... There was a false rumor that the government was going to designate this location as an official provincial park. That was why the villagers were a little disturbed. I also spear-headed the protest then... But we found out soon enough that the rumor was false, so it all ended pretty quickly and we all felt a little embarrassed by it."

Su-dong wiped the sweat off of his forehead. Now he regretted not burning all those placards instead of just throwing them away.

"I do have to consider what I've just seen, though," the man from Naju nodded gravely. "I have to think this all over."

He rolled up his car window then. Without another word, his car glided off into the distance, raising a cloud of dust as it went.

Su-dong stood there helplessly until the car disappeared beyond the embankment. He clenched his fist so hard that the bird began to cry.

When Su-dong trudged back to his house, he found his son playing with dirt in the yard and his wife nowhere to be seen.

"Here! Play with this, but be gentle so that it won't run away."

Su-dong handed the bird to his son. The child seemed afraid of it at first, but when Su-dong patted its feathers, his son shot his hands out to receive the bird.

"Geun-ho, would you like to go to Seoul with Mom and Dad?"

"Uh-huh."

"Then, you shouldn't go anywhere. Just play with this bird at home, okay?"

"Okay."

Su-dong patted his son on the cheeks and then

looked around the house. There was no trace of his wife taking care of the house. A rag was drying on the floor at random and his laundry for the last ten days was lying in a lump in the corner. It looked as if worms would crawl out of the kitchen gutter at any moment.

"Where's your mom?"

No answer. His son continued to play with the bird. Her shoes were in the entrance so his wife must have just been lying down in their room. She certainly was having a good time. She wasn't even on the lookout. He should have been the one just lying about. If she was coming back home after all this time shouldn't she back in the kitchen, scrubbing the floors and checking the refrigerator to see what had been rotting in it? Su-dong yanked his shoes off and threw the bedroom door open.

Something immediately smacked him in his face. The object tickled Su-dong's nose as it grazed its way down and Su-dong saw that it was a black gauze stocking that had been lumped together like a donut. That bitch. Su-dong knew exactly whose stocking it was. What the hell was she thinking she left something like that?

Su-dong just stood there not knowing how he

could salvage this situation. A piece of tissue paper imprinted with red rouge flew at his face next.

"You sent me and your son away to do this?" His wife was sitting beside her bag, unchanged and no more prepared to go than when he had left.

More than anything, Su-dong felt ashamed because he was squatting in front of his room and being humiliated like this in front of his own son.

"Are you out of your mind?" Su-dong decided to go back on the offensive. "Do you even have any idea what's even going on here? *Ho-pil's* been using this room. My God, you're driving me nuts!"

"Ho-pil...Ho-pil... You bastard! It was *her* shaking sesame in the garlic field! You, you're like an animal pretending to be a human..." She threw something else into his face again. This time it was something smaller. A crumpled up scrap of paper. It was damp with perspiration, probably because she had been holding it for a while. When he opened it...God... It was a bar receipt. Damnit all. That bitch must have served his wife at one point, too.

"It was a business..." But Su-dong stepped outside and closed the door after himself before even finishing his own sentence. His wife was grabbing at an ashtray. Luckily, she didn't throw it.

Stepping down to the yard, Su-dong asked his wife, "Did you pay her?" Her answer: "Do you think I'm crazy? If we have money to give her, why are we having such a hard time now?"

There was no point asking her how Miss Jeong was doing. If she was acting like this towards her own husband, that little lady must have really got it. She had probably been injured, at least. But, then, there was no telling how it had gone on between them. It looked as if the woman had also been quite resolute in facing his wife. She might have threatened his wife with a lawsuit. Then, she could have simply left after giving his wife advice on how to better control her husband. His wife, who became so crestfallen at the sound of the words "debt" and "law," might have just politely sent her away.

Su-dong went to the bathroom, removed his pants, and took a seat. He relaxed and felt a stream of diarrhea exit his bowels. Then he sighed and took his cigarette pack out of his pocket. He sighed again: nothing.

"Where did your ass of a daddy go?"

"I dunno."

He could hear his wife leave their bedroom and

enter the hall. Su-dong tried to clench and block the sound of his watery shit. He could hear his wife sighing deeply.

"Mom, what's the name of this bird?"

"I don't know. Ask your asshole of a dad! And you think now is the time to talk about some bird? You, son of a bunch of rotten bastards!"

She must have popped him in the head once; Su-dong could hear his son crying. That hot-tempered bitch! She was ruining their child completely.

"Stop crying! What do you think this kind of bird is? It's the kind of bird that'll bite off your pepper."

God—what had she just said? Su-dong sat down again with a muffled moan.

"A bird that'll bite my pepper off?" Su-dong's son repeated his mother, whimpering.

Su-dong's wife entered the kitchen, and Su-dong slipped into their bedroom. Treating the bag like a pillow, he lay down for a moment. Not only was he very tired from all the troubles he had had to deal with during the day, but he probably also needed a nap if he was going to drive to Seoul tonight.

He dozed off, but was rudely awakened by the sound of his son shrieking outside. His wife rushed out of the kitchen and began to yell. Su-dong turned around where he lay. He thought that this was worse than just living alone. Su-dong thought that he should probably get his wife under wraps at this point, but he barely managed to haul his tired body up and grab the door handle.

His son was sitting in the center of the yard crying. His pants were pulled halfway down his legs. Su-dong thought that he must have lost the bird while he pissed in the gutter. He didn't see the bird in either his son's or wife's hand.

His pants still hanging from the middle of his legs and gazing wide-eyed up at his mother, Su-dong's son said: "The bird just bit it and left." Then he resumed crying.

Su-dong's wife pulled up his pants quickly as if someone was about steal her son's penis.

"Good God, you little bastard! Why on earth did you show it to the bird, huh? Are you out of your mind?" Without any understanding why he had exposed himself to the bird, she began to scold him again. Su-dong felt like another smoke. And without even thinking about it, he pulled the ashtray full of cigarette butts towards himself.

Translated by Jeon Seung-hee

해설

Afterword

해학의 웃음으로 감싸는 작은 새의 숨결

정홍수 (문학평론가)

전성태는 한국소설의 리얼리즘적 전통에 충실한 가운데 자신만의 고유한 시선과 스타일을 구축해낸 작가이다. 그의 첫 소설집 『매향』(1999)은 70년대 산업화의 격변을 거쳐 세계 자본주의 질서 속으로 급속히 편입되던 8, 90년대 한국사회의 가장 낙후된 이면에 눈을 돌린다. 붕괴되는 농어촌이나 폐광촌의 현실이 그것인데, 작가는 밀려나는 세계에 대한 향수와 애도의 시선을 소설의 밑자락에 깔면서도 거기에 힘겹지만 의뭉스럽게 버티고 있는 사람살이의 활력과 깊은 속내를 놓치지 않는다. 그 만만치 않은 소설적 과제를 수행하는 과정에서 무엇보다 돋보이는 것은 작가의 적공(積功)을 짐작

A Small Bird's Breathing Embraced
by Humorous Laughter

Jeong Hong-su (literary critic)

Jeon Sung-tae has built his own unique style
while faithfully following the realist tradition char-
acteristic of modern Korean fiction. His first short
story collection *Incense Burial* (1999) focused on the
underside of 1980s and 1990s Korean society, the
side that fell behind farthest during the process of
global capitalist incorporation after the rapid indus-
trialization of the 1970s. Although Jeon mourns the
world's transformation—the destruction of the
countryside and fishing villages as well as the villages with their abandoned mines—with nostalgia,
he also does not miss the vitality latent in the depth
of so many people's difficult lives.

하게 하는 튼실한 언어이다. 전성태 소설의 언어는 그 적확함과 풍성함, 짜임새에서 기본적인 신뢰감을 주지만, 삶에 뿌리내린 토박이 향토어의 핍진한 구사를 통해 인물과 서사를 조형할 때 특히 빛난다. 그런데 이러한 향토어의 세계는 김유정, 이문구 등의 소설에서 보는 것처럼, 특정 방언의 단순한 채집과 배열을 넘어 그 말들에 스민 한국인의 신산(辛酸)과 해학을 포착하고 옮길 수 있을 때만 대체할 수 없는 소설적 표현에 이를 수 있다. 그런 점에서 90년대의 젊은 작가 전성태가 세대적·문화적 한계를 넘어 의뭉스럽고 깊은 향토어의 소설적 표현에서 상당한 성취를 보인 것은 놀랄 만한 일이다. 『매향』에 수록된 단편 「새」는 그 성취를 보여주는 뚜렷한 증좌이다. 이 작품에서 작가는 빚에 쪼들려 야반도주를 꿈꾸는 한 농촌 사내의 곤경을 그 지리멸렬함 속에서 우스꽝스럽게 그려내는데, 서사의 리듬에까지 스며들어 있는 남도 방언의 풍성함은 삶의 고단함을 받아내는 해학의 힘을 잘 보여준다. 그 해학과 웃음을 가능하게 하는 것은 벌어지고 있는 사태에 대한 일종의 거리감(距離感)이나 에두르는 시선이라 할 수 있을 텐데, 남도 방언의 의뭉스러움이 그 거리를 훌륭하게 감

What stands out the most in the author's attempt to carry out this difficult task is his solid body of language that suggests his years of hard work. We find Jeon Sung-tae's language reliable because of its precision, richness, and structure. Furthermore, his language shines when he constructs characters and narratives through vivid dialects rooted deeply in local native lives. These dialects can reach irreplaceable levels of novelistic achievement only when they go beyond simple collection and arrangement and proceed to capture and convey the hardships and humor steeped in their contexts, as illustrated in the writings of Kim Yu-jeong and Yi Mun-gu. In this sense, it is a pleasant surprise that Jeon Sung-tae, a young, 1990s author, could accomplish this remarkable level of dialectical achievement, overcoming both his generational and cultural limits.

"Bird," a short story included in *Incense Burial,* exemplifies this linguistic feat excellently. This story provides a humorous depiction of a man who plans to sneak away from his home village with his family because of his impossible debts. The richness of the Jeolla dialect saturated even in the narrative rhythms of the story illustrates the power of humor

당해내고 있다.

작품의 제목인 '새'부터가 그렇다. 소설의 주인공 장수동의 빚에 연대보증을 섰다가 낭패를 당하게 된 친구 호필은 수동이 도망칠까봐 트럭까지 압수해둔 상태이다. 그러나 호필은 아내를 데려와야겠다는 수동의 거짓말에 두말 않고 트럭 키를 내준다. 그러면서 풀새밭에서 잡았다며 작은 새 한 마리를 수동의 아들 근호에게 주라며 건네준다. 수동은 그 날개 묶인 작은 새에게서 빚에 몰려 도망칠 궁리만 하고 있는 자신의 처량한 처지를 본다. "니도 잘나가는 시절 다 가부렀다잉? 날 보그라. 니하고 다를 게 하나도 읎어야. 인자 살어갈 날개는 읎고 도망갈 날개만 남어부렀응께……." 그러나 이러한 감정의 투사에만 그쳤다면 '새'는 그저 진부한 상징에 머물고 말았을 것이다. 전성태의 '새' 이야기는 한 차원을 더 가지고 있다. 수동의 아내는 아들 근호를 야단칠 때마다 "고추 떨어진 딸내미로 안 태어나고 사내아이로 태어났느냐며" 남편에 대한 원망까지 얹어 싸잡아 말하곤 했는데, 그러다보니 근호의 장래희망은 "따알(딸)"이 되는 것이다. 빚더미 와중에 단란주점 여자와 바람까지 피운 남편에게 화가 날 대로 나 있던 수동의

that allows people to withstand their hardships. The slyness of a southern dialect conveys the sense of distance towards the impossible plight, a sense of distance required to enable humor and laughter towards it.

The way the titular "bird," is used illustrates Jeon Sung-tae's excellent skills in mobilizing dialects. Jang Su-dong's friend, Ho-pil, confiscates Su-dong's truck to prevent him from running away after Ho-pil gets into serious trouble for co-signing Su-dong's loan. Even so, Ho-pil readily returns Su-dong his truck keys when Su-dong lies that he has to bring his runaway wife back. Along with the keys, Ho-pil gives Su-dong a small bird for Su-dong's young son, Geun-ho. In this small bird, its wings tied back, Su-dong sees his own pathetic situation, trapped and on run from his debts. Thus, Su-dong says to the bird, "The good old days are all gone for you too, huh? ...Look at me. I'm not all that different from you. I don't have wings to fly with or live on, just wings for running away..."

But if there were only this empathy for the bird, it would remain merely a stale symbol. There is another dimension to the bird's symbolic status in Jeon Sung-tae's story. Su-dong's wife habitually

아내는 새를 가지고 노는 아들 근호에게 남편의 행방을 묻다가 한숨을 내쉰다. 아이는 엄마에게 새 이름을 묻고, 기다렸다는 듯이 아내의 지청구가 시작된다. "몰러! 니 잘난 애비한테 물어봐라. (…) 뭐긴 뭐겠냐? 자지 물어갈 새제." "자지물어갈새?" 지금 수동은 아내를 피해 변소에 숨어서 이 대화를 듣고 있다. 소설의 마지막, 아이는 토방에 앉아 울고 있다. 아랫도리를 반이나 드러낸 채다. 새는 보이지 않는다. 아이는 제 어미를 올려다보며 울먹이며 말한다. "깨물어만 보고 기양 가부렀다." '고추' 없는 '따알'이 되고 싶었던 아이는 "자지 물어갈 새"라는 어미의 말에 자신의 '고추'를 새에게 내주려 했던 것이고, 그러다 새를 놓치고 만 것이다. 그 순간 놀란 아내는 아이의 바지를 추켜올려주며 야단을 친다. "워매, 썩을 놈! 뭔 지랄한다고 고것을 새한테 내보이냐!" 웃을 수도, 울 수도 없는 이 장면에서 소설은 끝난다. 우리는 '새'를 매개로 한 작은 소극에 웃음 짓는 가운데 이 지리멸렬한 가족이 어떻게든 지지고 볶으며 살아갈 수 있으리라는 생각을 품게 된다. '희망' 같은 거창한 말 없이도 그들은 살아갈 것이다. 밀려나고 배제되는 삶에 대한 작지만 따뜻한 긍정과 감싸안음. 전성태의 「새」는

curses their son "for being born male, crying why had he been born a boy, not a girl, a girl without that damn pepper," projecting her frustrations regarding her husband onto her son. Consequently, Geun-ho dream to become a "da-u-gh-ter." Later, furious with her husband who has not only run up huge debts but also slept with a bar hostess, Su-dong's wife answers her son's question regarding the bird's name with, "I don't know. Ask your asshole of a dad! [...] What do you think this kind of bird is? It's the kind of bird that'll bite off your pepper." The boy echoes his mother, "A bird that'll bite my pepper off?" All the while, Su-dong hears this conversation in the bathroom where he is hiding.

At the end of the short story, Su-dong's son is found sitting in the center of the yard crying. His pants are pulled halfway down his legs. The bird has disappeared and the tearful son says to his mother, "The bird just bit it and left." The son, who wanted to become a "da-u-gh-ter" without a "pepper," tried to give his "pepper" to the bird, after his mother told him it was "the kind of bird that'll bite off your pepper." Su-dong's wife, completely taken aback, pulls up their son's pants quickly and scolds him, "Good God, you little bastard! Why on

한때 '민중'이라는 이름으로 불렸던 바로 그들의 언어로 그 작은 새의 고단한 숨결을 감싼다. 고단함을 견디고 비껴가는 해학의 웃음과 함께.

earth did you show it to the bird, huh? Are you out of your mind?" The story ends with this scene where no one can simply cry or laugh. And, while laughing at this small farce revolving around a bird, we are left with the intimation that this chaotic family will somehow live on, that they will survive and soldier on even without a grand word like "hope."

Jeon Sung-tae's "Bird" embraces and abounds with affirmation for lives that have been pushed out and excluded. Jeon Sung-tae's "Bird" embraces that small, striving bird with the language of those who were once called *minjung*, and with a humor that enables them to withstand and weather their hardships.

비평의 목소리

Critical Acclaim

전통의 단호한 단절을 경험하고 있는 세기말의 지금, 전성태의 작품들이 보여주는 전통적 문체의 계승은 그만큼 어려운 작업일 테고 그래서 더욱 값진 것으로 판단된다. 구성력, 묘사력도 좋고 해학적 언어구사도 훌륭하다.

현기영

전성태의 작품에 나타난 향토어 지향의 담론은 단순히 특정 방언에 대한 혈연적 친밀성의 표현이라고 생각되지 않는다. 그것은 향토적 언어의 재미와 효과를 나름대로 치밀하게 계산한 언어수행임에 명백하며, 이는

In this turn-of-the-century present where we often experience the discontinuation of tradition, Jeon Sung-tae's continuation of a more traditional style must be an even more difficult task and therefore that much more precious than any time before. The structure, narrative style, and humorous language are all superb.

Hyun Ki-young

The dialect-oriented discourse in Jeon Sung-tae's literature is not a simple result of his native affinity with a certain regional dialect. It is a linguistic performance, based on thoughtful calculation of the

말의 예술적 분절(articulation)이란 수준에서 평가할 만
한 것이다.

황종연

전성태의 첫 소설집『매향』은 보기 드문 적공(積功)의
문학이다. 풍성한 한국어의 성찬을 거느린 정확한 문장
들은 작가의 오랜 연마를 느끼게 하기에 충분하다. 자
연과 삶의 구석구석에 드리우는 눈길의 진득함은 농촌
생활의 작은 삽화들에서 인간사의 단면을 적출해내는
탄탄한 구성력으로 튼실하게 전화되어 있다. 1990년대
들어와 여러모로 심하게 도전받고 있는 한국소설의 리
얼리즘 전통을 답답할 정도로 잇고 있는 모습도 시류의
저편에서 문학과 사람살이의 긴 호흡을 담아내려는 쉽
지 않은 미덕이다. 이 미덕은 김유정으로부터 이문구에
이르는 걸진 해학의 언어로부터, 황석영의 초기 단편들
을 방불케 하는 견고한 서정의 리얼리즘까지 한국 근현
대 소설의 빛나는 전통에 고개 숙여 세례받은 겸손과
적공의 우보(牛步)인 것처럼 보인다.

정홍수

joy and effect regional dialects can bring to a story. We should evaluate its effect on the plane of artistic articulation of a language.

Hwang Jong-yeon

Jeon Sung-tae's *Incense Burial* is a rare achievement resulting from years of dedicated labor. We can sense the years of training in his concise sentences that offer a feast of rich Korean language. Various sketches of a country life representative of a wider society support his steady gaze of even the tiniest corners of our environment and lives. It is Jeon Sung-tae's unusual virtue to succeed, almost too faithfully to some, the realist tradition of Korean fiction, which had been seriously challenged on various fronts throughout the 1990s. Jeon's work demonstrates his status as a writer with a far-sighted vision of our lives and literature, a writer above trends. His virtues appear to be the result of modesty and a steady effort, and seem to be based on a respect for the brilliant tradition of modern Korean fiction, from the humorous language of Kim Yu-jeong and Yi Mun-gu to the solid lyrical realism of Hwang Sok-yong's early short stories.

Jeong Hong-su

전성태의 변모는 주목할 만하다. 빼어난 언어 구사력과 세밀한 묘사력이 일품이되 향토적 사실주의의 한계를 시원하게 넘어서지 못했던『매향』의 전성태가 우리 시대 삶의 여러 경계를 성찰하는 비범한 예술가로 변모한 것이다. 두 번째 소설집『국경을 넘는 일』에 수록된「존재의 숲」은 이러한 놀라운 변모 이면에서 그가 어떤 예술적 경계를 돌파했는지를 보여주는 동시에 오늘날 사실주의 문학의 한계와 가능성을 예리하게 짚는 뜻 깊은 작품이다. "말이 입에 올랐으되 삶을 밟고 있지는 못한 형국"에 처한 개그맨 화자에게 점쟁이가 들려주는 충고의 핵심은 '캄캄한 삶'을 밟아보라는 것인데, 이는 '진창에 구르며' 밑바닥 삶을 겪는 것과 다르다. 점쟁이는 오히려 그런 경우에 생기는 "자기연민은 공연히 억지가 되기 십상"임을 지적한다. 오늘날 사실주의 문학의 문제점을 이보다 예리하게 짚기는 힘들 것이다.

한기욱

전성태는 과작의 작가이다. 등단 6년 만에 첫 작품집을 묶었고, 15년이 넘도록 겨우 소설집 세 권과 장편소

Jeon Sung-tae's transformation is noteworthy. The writer of *Incense Burial,* where Jeon's linguistic mastery and elaborate descriptions stand out, yet seem to be somewhat imprisoned in provincial realism, is transformed into the extraordinary sort of artist capable of pondering deeply about the various borders in our lives. "Forest of Being," included in his second short story collection *How to Cross Over the National Border*, is a significant work of art that shows what artistic borders he has crossed to make this surprising transformation while suggesting the limits and potential of today's realist literature. The gist of the fortuneteller's advice to the narrator, who is lost in a "situation in which words are on his lips, but his feet are not firmly on the ground of his life," is that he should walk the "dark life." This does not mean that the fortuneteller advises him to simply experience a life of penury, a life "rolling in mud." On the contrary, the fortuneteller warns him that one's self-pity, often natural in this sort of situation, might be an irrational hindrance to his growth. It would be hard for anyone to come up with a formula that points out the problems in today's realist literature more succinctly than this.   Han Gi-uk

설 한 권을 냈을 뿐이다. 그러나 이 저조한 생산력은 유별난 게으름의 소치라기보다 작가적 결벽증의 산물일 것이다. 치밀한 구성과 안정된 문장 때문에 전성태는 일단 믿고 즐길 수 있는 작가라고 할 수 있다. 소재와 주제의 진화가 뚜렷하며, 더디지만 침착하게 내딛는 행보에는 일관성이 있다. 『매향』에서 공동체적 삶에 대한 향수와 몰락의 미학으로 시작한 그 행보는 『국경을 넘는 일』을 기점으로 개인과 사회, 실존과 역사의 조화라는 고전적인(또한 당대적인) 주제로 확장되고, 2009년 한국 소설의 중요한 성과로 기억될 세 번째 소설집 『늑대』에서는 개인의 정체성 형성에 개입하는 이데올로기적 기제에 대한 집요한 탐색으로 깊어진다. 『늑대』의 전반부에는 표제작을 비롯해 작가의 몽골 체류 경험이 투영된 '몽골 연작' 여섯 편이 실려 있다. 소설 공간의 확장이라는 차원에서 전성태의 몽골은 방현석의 베트남, 정도상의 중국, 배수아의 독일, 오수연의 팔레스타인 등과 더불어 2000년대 한국 소설이 새롭게 발견한 시공간에 속한다. 이 시공간은 다양한 경계를 횡단하는 최근 소설의 지배적 경향의 일부이며, 국경을 넘나드는 세계화 시대에 타자와의 만남을 통해 자기 성찰의 계기를 포착

Jeon Sung-tae is not a prolific writer. His first short story collection came out six years after his literary debut, and he has produced only three short story collections and a novel over his near fifteen-year career. This low level of output is not due to the writer's laziness, though, but to his fastidiousness. Thanks to the flawless structure and pristine individual sentences of his writing, Jeon Sung-tae is an author we can be sure to enjoy. His characters and themes progress clearly and his plots always advance slowly, but steadily. Jeon's exploratory trajectory began with a sense of nostalgia about the communal lives and the aesthetics of decline in *Incense Burial*, expanded to the classic (or contemporary) theme of the harmony between individual and society, or between existence and history in *How to Cross Over the National Border*, and continued to the study of the ideological mechanisms involved in an individual's identity formation in *The Wolf*, his third short story collection and a critical Korean literary achievement in 2009. In the first half of *The Wolf*, there are six Mongol series stories, reflecting the author's time in Mongolia. Along with Bang Hyun-seok's Vietnam, Jeong Do-sang's China, Bae Su-ah's Germany, and Oh Su-

하려는 문제의식을 공유한다.

진정석

yeon's Palestine, Jeon Sung-tae's Mongolia is a new chronotope of Korean fiction of the 2000s. This chronotope of Mongolia is a part of newly emerging trend in contemporary fiction to cross borders. It shares with other chronotopes the intention to reflect on oneself through encounters with others in the globalizing contemporary world.

Jin Jeong-seok

전성태

작가 전성태는 1969년 전남 고흥에서 태어났다. 1989
년 중앙대학교 예술대학 문예창작학과에 입학해서는
문예 동아리 '진군나팔'에 가입하여 졸업 때까지 활동했
고, 학생회장 이내창이 의문의 죽음을 당하자 진상규명
투쟁에 참여했다. 1990년 군에 입대하여 강원도 화천의
포병부대에서 복무했다. 전역 후 복학하여 2004년 제1
회 실천문학신인상 공모에 단편 「닭몰이」가 당선되면
서 문단에 나왔다. 1999년 고향을 찾았다가 거금도에서
전설적인 레슬러 김일을 만났다. 이 만남은 이듬해 단
편 「퇴역 레슬러」(2000)를 쓰는 계기가 되었다. 첫 소설
집 『매향』(실천문학사, 1999)을 출간하고, 신동엽문학상을
수상했다. 2005년 9월부터 이듬해 봄까지 6개월간 몽골
울란바토르에서 체류했다. 두 번째 소설집 『국경을 넘
는 일』(창비, 2005), 장편소설 『여자 이발사』(창해, 2005)를
출간했다. 2007년 세 번째 소설집 『늑대』(창비)를 출간하
고, 이 소설집으로 채만식문학상(2009), 무영문학상
(2010), 올해의 작가상(2010)을 받았다. 2010년 산문집

Jeon Sung-tae

Jeon Sung-tae was born in Goheung, Jeollanam-do in 1969. After entering the Department of Creative Writing at Chungang University, he joined the literary circle, "A Marching Trumpet," of which he was an active member until he graduated. However, when his university's student council president, Yi Nae-chang was found dead for unknown reasons, he decided to join in the students' fight to discover the truth. In 1990, he enlisted for his compulsory military service in an artillery unit in Hwacheon, Gangwon-do. After being discharged in 1993, he enrolled in college again. He made his literary debut by winning the *Silcheonmunhak* New Writer's Award for his short story "Chicken Beating" in 2004. In 1999, he encountered the legendary wrestler Kim Il in Geogeumdo during his visit to his home town. This encounter inspired him to write "Retired Wrestler" the following year. In 1999, his first short story collection, *Incense Burial,* came out in Silcheonmunhaksa and, in 2000, he received the 18th Shin Dong-yeop Creative Writing Fund Award.

『성태 망태 부리봉태』를 출간했다. 2011년 단편소설「국화를 안고」로 오영수문학상을, 2012년 단편「낚시하는 소녀」로 현대문학상을 수상했다. 현재 충남 천안시에 거주하며 전업작가로 활동하고 있다.

Starting from 2005, Jeon began to live with his family in Ulaanbaatar, Mongolia. He lived there for six months, from September 2005 until the spring of 2006. His third short story collection *The Wolf* came out shortly after this period in 2007, winning him the 6th Chae Man-sik Literary Award (2009), the 11th Muyeong Literary Award (2010) and the Writer of the Year Award (2009). His first essay collection, *Sungtae Mangtae BuriBungtae*, was published in 2010. He won the 19th Oh Yeong-su Literary Award for short story "Chrysanthemum in her Arms" in 2011, and won the 57th *Hyundae Munhak* Magazine Award for the short story "A Girl, Fishing" in 2012. Currently, he resides in Cheonan, Chungcheongnam-do where he continues to write.

번역 **전승희** Translated by Jeon Seung-hee

전승희는 서울대학교와 하버드대학교에서 영문학과 비교문학으로 박사 학위를 받았으며, 현재 하버드대학교 한국학 연구소의 연구원으로 재직하며 아시아 문예 계간지 《ASIA》 편집위원으로 활동 중이다. 현대 한국문학 및 세계문학을 다룬 논문을 다수 발표했으며, 바흐친의 『장편소설과 민중언어』, 제인 오스틴의 『오만과 편견』 등을 공역했다. 1988년 한국여성연구소의 창립과 《여성과 사회》의 창간에 참여했고, 2002년부터 보스턴 지역 피학대 여성을 위한 단체인 '트랜지션하우스' 운영에 참여해 왔다. 2006년 하버드대학교 한국학 연구소에서 '한국 현대사와 기억'을 주제로 한 워크숍을 주관했다.

Jeon Seung-hee is a member of the Editorial Board of *ASIA*, and a Fellow at the Korea Institute, Harvard University. She received a Ph.D. in English Literature from Seoul National University and a Ph.D. in Comparative Literature from Harvard University. She has presented and published numerous papers on modern Korean and world literature. She is also a co-translator of Mikhail Bakhtin's *Novel and the People's Culture* and Jane Austen's *Pride and Prejudice*. She is a founding member of the Korean Women's Studies Institute and of the biannual Women's Studies' journal *Women and Society* (1988), and she has been working at 'Transition House,' the first and oldest shelter for battered women in New England. She organized a workshop entitled "The Politics of Memory in Modern Korea" at the Korea Institute, Harvard University, in 2006. She also served as an advising committee member for the Asia-Africa Literature Festival in 2007 and for the POSCO Asian Literature Forum in 2008.

감수 **데이비드 윌리엄 홍** Edited by David William Hong

데이비드 윌리엄 홍은 미국 일리노이주 시카고에서 태어났다. 일리노이대학교에서 영문학을, 뉴욕대학교에서 영어교육을 공부했다. 지난 2년간 서울에 거주하면서 처음으로 한국인과 아시아계 미국인 문학에 깊이 몰두할 기회를 가졌다. 현재 뉴욕에서 거주하며 강의와 저술 활동을 한다.

David William Hong was born in 1986 in Chicago, Illinois. He studied English Literature at the University of Illinois and English Education at New York University. For the past two years, he lived in Seoul, South Korea, where he was able to immerse himself in Korean and Asian-American literature for the first time. Currently, he lives in New York City, teaching and writing.

바이링궐 에디션 한국 대표 소설 057

새

2014년 3월 7일 초판 1쇄 인쇄 | 2014년 3월 14일 초판 1쇄 발행

지은이 전성태 | 옮긴이 전승희 | 펴낸이 김재범
감수 데이비드 윌리엄 홍 | 기획 정은경, 전성태, 이경재
편집 정수인, 이은혜 | 관리 박신영 | 디자인 이춘희
펴낸곳 (주)아시아 | 출판등록 2006년 1월 27일 제406-2006-000004호
주소 서울특별시 동작구 서달로 161-1(흑석동 100-16)
전화 02.821.5055 | 팩스 02.821.5057 | 홈페이지 www.bookasia.org
ISBN 979-11-5662-002-0 (set) | 979-11-5662-014-3 (04810)
값은 뒤표지에 있습니다.

Bi-lingual Edition Modern Korean Literature 057

Bird

Written by Jeon Sung-tae | **Translated by** Jeon Seung-hee
Published by Asia Publishers | 161-1, Seodal-ro, Dongjak-gu, Seoul, Korea
Homepage Address www.bookasia.org | **Tel**. (822).821.5055 | **Fax**. (822).821.5057
First published in Korea by Asia Publishers 2014
ISBN 979-11-5662-002-0 (set) | 979-11-5662-014-3 (04810)

〈바이링궐 에디션 한국 대표 소설〉 작품 목록(1~45)

도서출판 아시아는 지난 반세기 동안 한국에서 나온 가장 중요하고 첨예한 문제의식을 가진 작가들의 작품들을 선별하여 총 105권의 시리즈를 기획하였다. 하버드 한국학 연구원 및 세계 각국의 우수한 번역진들이 참여하여 외국인들이 읽어도 어색함이 느껴지지 않는 손색없는 번역으로 인정받았다. 이 시리즈는 세계인들에게 문학 한류의 지속적인 힘과 가능성을 입증하는 전집이 될 것이다.

바이링궐 에디션 한국 대표 소설 set 1

바이링궐 에디션 한국 대표 소설 set 2